HER READY-MADE FAMILY

BY
JESSICA HART

MILLS & BOON®

For Isabel, with love

First published in Great Britain 2006
Large Print edition 2006
Harlequin Mills & Boon Limited,
Eton House, 18-24 Paradise Road,
Richmond, Surrey TW9 1SR

© Jessica Hart 2006

ISBN-13: 978 0 263 19013 7
ISBN-10:   0 263 19013 7

Set in Times Roman 16½ on 18¼ pt.
16-1006-57615

Printed and bound in Great Britain
by Antony Rowe Ltd, Chippenham, Wiltshire

CHAPTER ONE

ALISTAIR eyed the dog on the table and sighed. It was obviously one of those days.

It had started with an early morning call out to one of Jim Marsh's heifers that was having trouble calving, and gone steadily downhill from then on. He hadn't been able to save the calf, and had returned home at last to find a particularly unpleasant email from his ex-wife Shelley, threatening a visit. He'd been bitten by a gerbil, scratched by a rabbit, pecked by a goose, kicked by a horse and had had to put a much-loved cat to sleep.

And frankly the last thing he felt like doing now was dealing with a pampered pooch in a jewelled collar.

Or rather, with its neurotic owner.

Alistair's jaundiced gaze travelled to the owner in question. He had to admit that she didn't *look* the neurotic type. She was tall and slender, with dark glossy hair and a strong face that was striking rather than pretty, and she was immaculately, if inappropriately, dressed in soft suede trousers, pointy boots and a silk shirt. She looked cool, intelligent, stylish and absurdly out of place in this plain country surgery.

Not the kind of woman one could imagine owning a dog at all, let alone putting it in a pink collar studded with *faux* diamonds, but if Alistair had learnt one thing in his years as a vet, it was that people were funny about their animals.

He turned his attention back to the dog, who peered nervously back at him through its shaggy fringe. Tallulah, she had said it was called. What kind of name was that for a dog? Alistair wondered irritably.

'There's nothing wrong with this dog that some decent exercise won't cure, Mrs…er…' Alistair glanced at the computer screen to remind himself of the woman's surname, and her strong dark brows snapped together.

'It's *Ms*,' said Morgan sharply. She hated the way people insisted on labelling women by their marital status at the best of times, and right now, when her own marital status, or lack of it, was such a sore point, she didn't feel like being laid back about the issue.

She saw the vet lift his brows at her apparent sensitivity. He didn't exactly roll his eyes, but she could tell that he felt like it, and she set her teeth.

'I'm Morgan Steele,' she said, wondering if he would recognize her.

He didn't. There was not so much as a flicker in the coolly assessing grey eyes.

Morgan didn't know whether to be pleased or miffed about that. She wasn't exactly a celebrity, but her name was fairly well-known, and there *had* been an interview with her in the local paper after all.

Not that this Alistair Brown probably read anything but *Calf Castrators' Weekly,* she thought, eyeing him with a shade of resentment. She had hoped to find a cheerful, kindly country vet like the ones you saw on television, but this one didn't seem the least bit cheerful or particularly kindly. Instead, he had a nondescript face rescued from blandness by acute eyes, a stern mouth and an air of badly concealed impatience.

'Well, *Ms* Steele,' he said caustically, 'I can tell you that your dog is verging on obese.' He prised

Tallulah's jaws gently apart to peer at her teeth, and then ran his hands over her tubby body once more. With a different owner, she would have been a nice, sturdy little Westie but as it was she had been completely ruined.

'It's a form of cruelty to let an animal get this overweight,' he told Morgan in a crisp voice. 'You shouldn't have a dog unless you're prepared to look after it properly.'

Morgan bridled at his tone. It was a very long time since anyone had dared to speak to her like that, and she didn't like it one little bit.

'Tallulah's my mother's dog,' she said, tight-lipped. 'She would have been horrified at the suggestion that she was cruel in any way. My mother was very attached to her.'

'Not attached enough to take her for a walk,' said Alistair, shaking a thermometer and inserting it under Tallulah's tail, ignoring the dog's yelp of surprise and discomfort.

Morgan averted her eyes. She bet that thermometer was cold.

'My mother was ill for the last couple of years,' she found herself explaining, although she didn't see why she should have to justify herself to him. 'She could hardly walk herself, so Tallulah was a wonderful companion for her. When my mother died a few months ago I took her to live with me.'

'There's nothing wrong with your legs, though, is there?' Alistair said pointedly.

He could see for himself that there wasn't. They were, in fact, spectacular legs, he found himself thinking as his eyes travelled up from the smart pointed boots.

'You could have given the dog some exercise,' he pointed out as he withdrew the thermometer to Tallulah's evident relief and squinted at it for a moment. 'It must have been obvious that's what she needed.'

'Tallulah doesn't like walking,' said Morgan defensively. 'She hates the rain and can't bear getting her paws muddy. She's not really a country dog.'

'Evidently,' said Alistair, and the dry note in his voice made Morgan flush. His eyes rested on her silk shirt and suede trousers. 'And not really a country owner either, is that it?'

'No, that is *not* it!' snapped Morgan, more ruffled than she cared to admit by that ironic grey gaze. 'I happen to be making my home here. There's no law that says you have to wear green wellies and a Barbour in the country, is there?'

'It's not a law but, given the weather here, it's certainly more practical than what you're wearing at the moment!'

Morgan sucked in her breath and counted to ten. She had faced down boardrooms and impatient investors and hostile journalists and she was *not* going to let some country vet make her lose her cool.

'I'm sorry you don't approve of my wardrobe,' she said icily, 'but I didn't come here for fashion advice. My dog has been wheezing and panting for the last couple of days and she seems in some distress, so perhaps you could do a little less criticizing and a little more diagnosing?'

Most people quailed when Morgan spoke to them like that, but not Alistair Brown.

'I've done my diagnosis,' he said, facing her across the table where Tallulah stood with her tail miserably down, her fat body shivering with nerves, and his voice was as cold as hers. 'You're welcome to go elsewhere for a second opinion, but I can tell you what any decent vet is going to tell you. The dog is seriously overweight and needs to go on a strict diet for a start.'

'A diet?' Morgan felt as if she should cover Tallulah's ears. Her mother had constantly fed the dog little titbits and insisted that she had a whole gingernut at coffee time.

'I'll give you some special dried food to give her,' Alistair was saying. 'You'll have to make sure there's plenty of fresh drinking water available, but don't give her anything else.'

Morgan's heart sank. 'She hates that stuff. She won't eat it.'

'She will if she's hungry,' he said brutally.

He felt Tallulah all over once more, and Morgan was annoyed to find herself thinking how strong and capable his hands looked. She fixed her eyes on his face instead, but that wasn't much better as she only started noticing the determined set of his jaw and the cool, quiet but somehow disturbing line of his mouth.

'There's nothing much wrong with you apart from the excess weight,' he told the dog, and fondled her ears for a moment before lifting his eyes to Morgan once more.

His gaze was sharp and light, and, caught unawares by its piercing effect, Morgan's heart gave a stupid little lurch.

'Stick to the diet I've prescribed—no treats!— and see if you can shift some of that weight by taking her for at least one good walk every day.

No tottering down to the end of the road and back,' he said, as if reading Morgan's mind. 'I suggest you find yourself a pair of wellies and be prepared to get dirty!'

Morgan's heart, having only just settled back into place after that odd little jerk of excitement, set off into action once more, this time in a distinctly downward motion.

Alistair read her dismayed expression without difficulty. 'Look, it'll only take an hour out of your day. Surely you can spare that?' he said, irritation threading his voice. 'I presume you care about the dog or you wouldn't have brought her here?'

Morgan looked at the quivering dog on the table. The truth was that she had never had much time for Tallulah. Her mother had been frankly silly about her pets, and treated them as if they were children, an affectation that Morgan had always found more than a little embarrassing—and annoying when they turned out, as Tallulah had done, to be greedy, spoilt and badly behaved.

'I feel responsible for her,' she conceded. 'I'd be lying if I said I was fond of her, but I promised my mother I'd look after her, so that's what I'm doing.'

'Well, *be* responsible then,' said Alistair

brusquely. 'She could be a nice little dog if you looked after her properly.' The cold grey gaze swept over Morgan, taking in her carefully groomed appearance, the subtle make-up and polished nails. 'Give her a fraction of the attention you give yourself, and bring her back in a month,' he said. 'We'll see if you're still wearing those boots then.'

Morgan was seething with rage and embarrassment as she wrote out a cheque for the fresh-faced veterinary nurse who was manning the reception desk. On top of everything else, it appeared that she had to pay through the nose for the privilege of being insulted and humiliated by the local vet.

So much for country life! Morgan had never had any reason to go to a vet in London, but she was sure that they were charming compared to Alistair Brown, who had obviously taken lessons in how to be a dour Yorkshireman.

'We'll show him!' she told Tallulah, hefting her into the front passenger seat. 'We'll come back in a month and you're going to be so trim and fit he won't recognize you—*and* I'll wear my boots!'

How dared he suggest that she was irresponsible? Morgan scowled as she got into her car and slammed the door shut. She wanted to shout at him that she had spent her whole life being responsible and she was sick of it.

She had looked after her mother, and Minty, and her friends, and her employees, and even her mother's *dog*, and now, just when it seemed she had a chance to look after herself for a change, some country bumpkin vet presumed to suggest that *she* was irresponsible!

She didn't want to go for long hearty walks over the moors. She didn't want to get wet and tired and dirty, or to starve Tallulah and listen to her whimpering for her gingernut, but because Mr High-and-Mighty Alistair Brown had decreed that it would be irresponsible not to, she was going to have to do it all anyway.

'Relax,' her twin sister, Minty, was always telling her. 'The trouble with you, Morgan, is that you think you're the only one who can do anything. You should chill out a bit and let everyone else sort out their own problems.'

Minty hadn't wanted Morgan to take Tallulah. 'She'll just become a substitute child, and you'll end up one of those batty old spinsters who wear tweed and battered hats and talk to dogs as if they're people,' she said. 'If you're not careful, you'll start calling yourself Tallulah's *mummy*, and what will that do to your reputation as a tough, successful businesswoman?'

'I've spent years telling Mum to treat Tallulah like a dog instead of a baby,' Morgan protested. 'As you've just pointed out, I'm a tough businesswoman. I'm hardly likely to start doting on a dog now, am I?'

'Who knows what you'll do now you're moving to the country?' said Minty unhelpfully. 'Anyway, you're not as tough as you pretend to be. If you were, you'd have found another home for Tallulah, or had her put down.'

'I couldn't do that,' said Morgan, shocked. 'I promised Mum we'd look after her.'

'There you go. I told you that you weren't tough.'

'Look, you take her then,' said Morgan crossly.

'I can't. You know Sam's allergic to her.'

'Then it looks as if it's going to be me, then, doesn't it?'

Somehow it always ended up being her, Morgan thought.

She glanced down at the dog, who was still looking dejected. It couldn't have been a nice experience to be plonked on a table, felt all over by a cold-eyed man with hard hands, criticised for being fat and then have a thermometer shoved up your bottom.

Well, the feeling all over bit might not be too bad, Morgan amended, remembering how strong and sure his hands had looked. She would pass on the criticism and the thermometer, though.

It was all very well for Minty to tell her to leave everyone else to sort themselves out, but how could she do that with Tallulah?

'You're not going to put yourself on a diet or take yourself off to the gym every day, are you?' she said to Tallulah, whose ears pricked up at the sound of her voice.

Oops, here she was talking to the dog already. Maybe Minty was right. It would be the tweed skirt and the battered hat next.

Perhaps eccentric spinsterhood was her fate after all.

At least the slimming of Tallulah would be a project, Morgan told herself as she started the car, and the engine broke into a low, throaty growl that never failed to give her pleasure. She might be hopeless at relationships but at least she was good at making money, enough anyway to buy this fabulous car. Morgan loved its sleek lines, its sumptuous leather upholstery and its leashed power.

No doubt Alistair Brown would say it was impractical for the country, but there was no way Morgan was giving it up. She might, after all, slope into Askerby and buy a pair of rubber boots, but she would draw the line at buying a sensible car. She might be trying to change her life, but there were limits.

It would certainly be a challenge to slim Tallulah down and train her to be a good country dog, but then she had always liked a challenge, Morgan reflected as she swung the car round and away from the surgery. She was good at identifying goals and meeting them. That had been the secret of her success so far, and there was no doubt that she was short of goals now that the house was finished.

Had it been a terrible mistake to move to Yorkshire? It had seemed such a good idea at the time. She had sold her business for an extraordinary amount of money, her mother had died, Paul had left…what better moment could there have been to change her life?

She had been sick of London then, sick of deadlines and tension and traffic. The simplicity and space of rural life had had an irresistible appeal after so many years in the rat race, and Morgan had imagined herself doing the things she had never had time to do before: to sit and read, to cook, to garden, to become part of a real community.

But if the community was composed of people like Alistair Brown, it wasn't going to be much fun. She hoped the other locals were going to be friendlier. It was a shame really that he was so brusque, Morgan mused, turning between the imposing gateposts at the end of her drive. There had been a certain steely attraction to him, she had to admit, but a smile or a kind word would have made such a difference to her today.

Oh, well.

At least she had a beautiful car and a beautiful home, Morgan told herself, stamping firmly on the wave of depression that threatened to wash over her. She was incredibly lucky.

The car purred under the avenue of lime trees and her heart lifted as always at the thought of the house waiting for her at the end of the drive. Ingleton Hall was a jewel of a Jacobean mansion that had gradually fallen into neglect until a fire had left the roof collapsed and the rooms blackened with soot. Too expensive to repair, it had lain empty and abandoned for nearly fifteen years, until Morgan had seen it and known at once that she wanted to restore it to its former glory.

Distracted by her thoughts, Morgan didn't at first see the two small figures labouring up the slight incline on their bikes until she was almost on top of them. She frowned slightly as she braked. They were a long way off the road.

Her window slid silently down. 'Are you lost?' she asked, coming up beside the two bikes.

They had wobbled to a halt at the sound of the car and now Morgan found herself looking into the faces of two girls, both pink and puffed after their energetic ride. They looked about ten or twelve to Morgan's inexperienced eyes, and were obviously twins.

They eyed her with curiosity. 'We're on our way to Ingleton Hall. We want to see Morgan Steele,' said one. 'Is that you?' she asked doubtfully.

'Yes,' said Morgan in surprise, wondering what on earth they wanted with her. 'I'm Morgan.'

'You don't look much like your picture,' said the second twin. She sounded disappointed. Digging around in her basket, she retrieved a newspaper cutting that Morgan recognized as being from *The Askerby & District Gazette* and she looked from the photograph to Morgan and back again. 'Yes, it's her,' she said to her sister.

It was Morgan's turn to feel a bit disappointed. She usually hated having her picture taken, but she hadn't minded that photo. It showed her in front of the house, her beaky features softened by shadows from the rose scrambling over the trellis, and was really quite flattering. Nearly as good as a smear of Vaseline on the lens, Morgan had decided.

Shame that the two girls evidently hadn't recognized the elegant, glamorous woman in the photo, she thought, resigned.

'Well, now we know who I am, who are you?' she asked.

'I'm Polly and this is Phoebe,' said the one who had first spoken. 'We're twins,' she added unnecessarily.

'So I see,' said Morgan.

They were very alike but not quite identical, unlike her and Minty, who had always looked so different that no one could ever believe that they were twins. Their fair hair was cut in a practical bob and their eyes behind their glasses were blue and knowing. They looked like two sharp cookies to Morgan who, having once been a very sharp cookie herself, felt a twinge of recognition.

'Do you live in the village?' she asked.

They nodded. 'We've cycled all the way,' said Phoebe. 'We wanted to ask you if we could interview you.'

Morgan wasn't sure what she had been expecting, but it wasn't that. She switched off the engine. '*Interview* me?' she echoed in surprise.

'For the school magazine,' said Polly.

'Well, that's very flattering,' said Morgan, taken aback, 'but why do you want to interview me?'

'We read about you in the *Gazette*,' said Phoebe. 'It said you're famous.'

'And rich,' Polly put in.

'So we thought we could write about you.'

They looked at her hopefully.

'I don't think my life would be very interesting for school kids,' Morgan pointed out. 'I don't do anything very exciting, and I don't know any celebrities.'

'Oh.' Their faces fell slightly. 'But the article said you had a pool in your house and everything.'

Polly made having your own swimming pool sound like the last word in glamour and Morgan was touched that they were so impressed. All her friends' children in London were alarmingly so-phisticated from a very early age. It would take a private jet, at least, not to mention an intimate friendship with the entire cast of *Friends*, to impress that lot.

'Yes, I've got a pool,' she said. 'Would you like to see it?'

'Yes, *please*,' they chorused.

'And can we interview you as well?' said Phoebe.

Morgan was already getting the sense that she was the more practical of the two girls, and she approved of the way Phoebe checked that she and her sister would be able to get what they had come for. There was a stubborn, determined look about the twins that suggested they were used to getting what they wanted.

Morgan recognized that too.

What harm could it do, after all? she asked herself. She had been looking for a way into the community, and perhaps this was it. After several bruising encounters with the media, she was normally very wary of interviews and had only agreed to the *Gazette* because the editor had stressed that their main interest was in the house rather than her.

But this was just a school magazine. A few proud parents might read it and be prepared to extend a welcome to her because of it. Who knew, even that grumpy vet might read it and wish he hadn't been quite so rude!

'All right,' she said to Phoebe. 'You're on.'

She offered them a lift in the car but they opted to cycle on up to the house, so Morgan drove ahead, hoping they would be sufficiently impressed. In her experience, children weren't much into architecture, but she loved Ingleton Hall so much she couldn't help wanting everyone else to appreciate it too.

She needn't have worried about the twins' reaction. They oohed and aahed in all the right places and were plainly deeply impressed by the wing which had been cleverly converted to accommodate a beautiful pool and a private gym.

Phoebe, it turned out, was a computer buff whose eyes shone at the sight of Morgan's study with its state-of-the-art technology, while Polly was much more interested in the pool and the grounds. 'This is a lovely house,' she sighed when they reached the terrace, her eyes on the parkland stretching idyllically away from the garden. 'You could keep ponies,' she said wistfully.

'I'm afraid I don't know how to ride,' said Morgan.

'My dad could teach you.'

Morgan murmured something non-committal. The truth was that she was more than a little nervous of farm animals like horses and cows. They looked nice from a distance, but when you got up close they were awfully…big. No doubt that Alistair Brown would take that as further evidence of how unsuited she was to country life.

They did the interview in the kitchen. Morgan gave them some squash and made herself a cup of tea, and they sat around the kitchen table.

'We thought you'd have servants,' Polly confided. 'You know, like a butler and a cook.'

Morgan could tell that she'd disappointed them. 'It seems a bit of a waste to have a cook just for me. I do have someone to help with the gardening and a cleaner who comes in once a week,' she offered.

'Mrs Bolton, we know,' said Phoebe, nodding. 'She babysits us sometimes. She told us how cool the house was. That's why we wanted to see it for ourselves.'

'Well, I hope you like it, now you're here?'

'Oh, yes,' Phoebe assured her. 'We'd really like to live somewhere like this, wouldn't we, Polly?'

Polly nodded vigorously. 'Unless it's haunted,' she said after a moment.

'It's not haunted,' said Phoebe with scorn. 'That's just a stupid story.' She turned to Morgan for confirmation. 'There's no such thing as ghosts, is there?'

'I don't believe in them,' Morgan admitted. She was haunted by memories of Paul sometimes, but she didn't think that would count.

'Still, I'd be afraid to live here on my own,' said Polly. 'Don't you get lonely?'

Ah, there was a question.

Morgan didn't think the girls would understand if she told them about the raw, gaping hole in her life since Paul had gone, about the constant ache in her heart and the terrible feeling of being alone in a bleak landscape wherever you were.

'Tallulah keeps me company,' she said lightly, sidestepping the question. 'She'll protect me from any ghosts.'

'Is that your dog?' Polly and Phoebe had been staring at Tallulah with ill-concealed distaste. 'She's awfully fat.'

'I know,' Morgan sighed. 'I've got to put her on a diet. You'd better not give her any of your biscuits.'

She'd thought the twins would succumb to Tallulah's begging. The dog had tried everything—soulful looks, sitting up on her back legs and stretching her front paws against their chairs, whimpering and sighing—but Phoebe and Polly were unimpressed.

'Our dad would sort you out,' Polly told her. 'He's really strict.'

'Is he strict with you?' Morgan asked.

'Yes.' They nodded in unison, but she didn't think they seemed unduly crushed.

'Shall we start the interview?'

It was decided that Phoebe would ask the questions they had prepared, while Polly was to write down the answers.

'OK.' Phoebe cleared her throat and rustled her piece of paper importantly. 'How old are you?'

Morgan was a little taken aback by the directness of the question, but then she should have realised that it would be like this and she gave a mental shrug. What did it matter anyway? Their article was hardly going to be picked up by *The Times* and beamed around the world.

And what was so bad about nearly being forty, after all?

'I'm thirty-nine,' she said firmly.

The girls exchanged a glance. 'That's the same age as our dad,' Polly offered. 'When's your birthday?'

'*I'm* asking the questions, Polly,' said Phoebe bossily before turning back to Morgan. 'When *is* your birthday?'

'September the third,' said Morgan meekly.

Polly wrote it down as Phoebe consulted the list again.

'Would you like to get married?'

This was getting more personal than Morgan had bargained for but, short of being rude to the two girls, she didn't quite see how she could refuse to answer.

'How do you know I'm not?' she asked, playing for time, and was surprised to see them both look aghast.

'But...it said in the *Gazette* that you were single!'

'You don't want to believe everything you read in the newspapers.'

'And Mrs Bolton said you weren't married,' Polly remembered.

Morgan was about to point out that she had only met Mrs Bolton twice, so she could hardly be called as an expert witness on her marital status, but then she remembered the last time she had decided to be economical with the truth—OK, to lie—about her single state.

She had so nearly made the most enormous fool of herself at that awful school reunion by inventing an adoring fiancé just to wipe the pitying smile off an old classmate's face. If Bethany had probed any deeper, she would have exposed Morgan as a pitifully sad and frustrated spinster, reduced to creating an imaginary lover to make herself interesting. Fortunately she hadn't had a chance to interrogate Morgan before they were interrupted, but Morgan still cringed at the very thought of how close she had come to humiliation. She would never have been able to keep the pretence up for long.

'I'm not married,' she admitted humbly. 'But it's always best to check these things rather than make assumptions.'

Phoebe and Polly looked at each other in relief. 'Not married,' Polly wrote down laboriously, underlining *not* several times.

'Why not?' asked Phoebe, ever practical.

Morgan sighed. If she knew the answer to that, life might have been a lot easier. Minty thought it was because she was too intimidating. Morgan herself thought that if the only available men she ever seemed to meet were wimpish enough to be intimidated by her, she wasn't interested in them anyway.

Paul hadn't been intimidated. But then Paul hadn't wanted to marry her.

'It just never happened,' she told the girls. 'I was never in the right place at the right time with the right man.'

'Maybe you'll find someone to marry here,' Phoebe suggested, and Morgan smiled.

'You don't think I'm too old to get married?'

'Thirty-nine is quite old,' they agreed, 'but sometimes people do get married when they're old. Our teacher got married last year, and she was *forty-seven*,' Polly added, obviously unable to imagine being quite that ancient.

'Well, maybe there's hope for me yet,' said Morgan.

Polly nudged Phoebe to go on with the questions.

Phoebe consulted her paper once more. 'What would you like your husband to be like?'

Like Paul, thought Morgan before she could help

herself, and she fought down a wash of familiar despair. She had to stop thinking about Paul. There was no point. It was over and she was back on her own again, the way she had always been.

'Well, let's see,' she said, mustering a smile. She didn't want the twins thinking that she was lonely and sad, even if she was. 'I'd like him to be funny and kind and loving and loyal...somebody I could talk to and have a good time with. A friend.'

Was it so much to ask? she wondered bleakly. It seemed as if it was.

'What about how he looks?' asked Phoebe with just a trace of anxiety. 'Does he have to be handsome?'

Paul was handsome. So handsome that Morgan had always found it hard to believe that he could really be interested in her. He had seemed too good to be true.

As, indeed, he was.

'Looks aren't as important as a nice personality,' she told them.

'Not important.' Polly mouthed the words as she made a note.

'Would you mind marrying someone who had children?' Phoebe continued casually.

Morgan considered. 'I don't know very much

about children,' she said, thinking that this was the most personal interview that she had ever given. But hell, she'd started it, so she might as well carry on. 'I wouldn't object to stepchildren on principle, anyway.'

Out of the corner of her eye she saw Polly writing down 'woodnt object on principal'.

'Good,' said Phoebe, and there was a pause while they both beamed at her.

'Is that it?' Morgan asked after a moment. 'Don't you need anything else for your article?'

Polly looked at Phoebe and Phoebe looked at Polly, both apparently realising that their research was a bit thin.

'Um…do you like living in Ingleton?' asked Polly, suddenly inspired.

'I've only been here a week,' she admitted. 'I haven't really got to know anybody yet.' Apart from one grumpy vet. 'I'm sure I will like it here, though.'

Whatever Alistair Brown thought.

'I'm going to start by exploring more of the country round here,' she went on. 'I need to find somewhere I can walk Tallulah for a start.'

'We could show you some walks,' Phoebe said eagerly. 'We know lots, don't we, Polly?'

'Well…that's kind of you,' said Morgan, 'but your parents might not want you going off with a perfect stranger. You'd better check with them first.'

'You could come to tea,' said Polly. 'Then you wouldn't be a stranger.'

Morgan couldn't help smiling. 'Tea would be lovely, but you'll need to talk to your mother first.'

'She's in Spain. Our dad looks after us.'

'Oh.' Was that what all those personal questions had been about? Morgan wondered suddenly. Surely these two couldn't be matchmaking…could they? She wasn't at all a maternal type and she couldn't imagine herself having much in common with a divorced father of two. Whatever she'd said about not objecting to the idea of stepchildren, she didn't think she'd make a very good stepmother. A relationship where everything centred around the children frankly held little appeal for Morgan.

But the girls were so keen for her to come that she didn't have the heart to refuse. It would only be a cup of tea after all, and if it was awkward she could always make her excuses and go.

'Come on Saturday,' urged Phoebe. 'Dad

won't mind. He likes it when we invite friends to the house.'

Some of Morgan's suspicions subsided. She was touched at being considered the twins' friend. Perhaps that was how their father would think of her too. Not all the locals could be as sneery as Alistair Brown, surely.

'All right. As long as you check that it's all right with him, I'll come and have tea with you then.'

CHAPTER TWO

THE house felt very empty when Morgan had waved the twins off and watched them pedal out of sight down the long drive. Disconsolately, she turned back into the house and wandered through the beautiful rooms she had put so much time into creating.

For once the tranquil house failed to soothe her. She felt restless and dispirited, and guilty about feeling that way when she had so much to be positive about. She had worked hard to build up her software business into a multi-award-winning company that had just been bought out for a fantastic sum. She would never have to work again if she didn't want to, and she had the financial security she had craved ever since she had watched her mother struggle alone to bring up her two daughters. She had achieved her dream, in fact.

What she hadn't bargained for was the nagging sense of 'now what?' that came from realising that you had nothing to work for anymore.

'You're just having a mid-life crisis,' Minty had said when Morgan tried to explain this to her. 'You're coming up to the big four-oh. It's a classic time to stop and take stock of your life.'

'You're not taking stock,' Morgan objected. 'And if I'm going to be forty, you are too!'

'Having three children doesn't leave a lot of time for soul-searching,' Minty pointed out. 'Besides, I had to go through all that when Rick left. I didn't have much choice then but to reassess my life, but you haven't had to do that. You've just carried on working and making money, and it's only now you've got time to think about what really you want.'

'I've got what I want. I *have*,' she insisted as Minty raised a disbelieving eyebrow. 'I wanted success and financial security, and I've got both.'

'Oh, money,' said Minty dismissively. 'What about a successful relationship and emotional security?'

Morgan sighed. 'I know, I'm a big, fat failure on that front.'

'The trouble with you, Morgan, is that you

don't like failing. You've always been successful at whatever you do, but you've never got the
relationship thing, have you? You just treat it
like another goal that you focus on and throw all
your energies into, but relationships don't work
like that. You can't treat them like business plans,
or do it all by yourself.

'A successful relationship is always going to
take two,' Minty went on. 'You assume that
you're the only one that can make things right, so
you get on and sort out problems before anyone
else has had a chance to see what they can do, but
you can't deal with emotions like that. You need
to learn to sit back and see what happens.'

'I let it happen with Paul, and look where
that got me!'

'Paul's not the only man in the world. There's
someone else out there for you, Morgan. I think
you should go out and find him, and when you
do, don't treat him like a project that has to be
successfully completed on time. Just relax and
enjoy being in love.'

Fine, thought Morgan, remembering the conversation with her twin as she swam her custom-
ary forty laps of her exquisite pool. It was all
very well for Minty to say go out and find a man,

but where? She had changed her life, moved to a different part of the country, and the only man she had met had been charmless and unfriendly and not even attractive.

Well, not particularly attractive, anyway, she amended, recalling Alistair Brown's unnerving eyes and the uncompromising line of his mouth. OK if you went for the cool, brusque type, but hardly someone who would bowl you over even then.

Morgan went to bed feeling depressed that night, but when she woke up the sun was shining for once and she felt invigorated with a new sense of purpose.

It was time for her to get a grip. She just wasn't the kind of person who fell into a decline and got depressed. If she saw a problem, she solved it, so there was no reason she shouldn't do the same now.

So, thought Morgan, setting her elaborate espresso machine in action, what was her problem?

That was easy. Her problem was feeling lonely and unsettled and a failure at relationships.

Solution? Start a relationship and make it succeed.

Now all she needed was to work out how to do that. Perhaps she could try advertising in the *Gazette's* lonely hearts column, Morgan mused as the coffee machine started its alarming bubbling and gurgling repertoire. What could she say? *Strong, successful millionairess seeks man to help her feel less of a failure. No wimps (or vets) need apply.*

Or perhaps not.

No, what she needed to do was to get out and meet people. Specifically, men. And be charming and soft and vulnerable and not intimidate them. Everyone else seemed to be able to do it. Why couldn't she?

She *could* do it, Morgan told herself. She would just have to try harder.

And her first step towards the solution was to get out there and meet as many people as possible. She had already accepted the invitation to join the Board of Governors at the village primary school, and she had tea with Polly and Phoebe and their abandoned father to look forward to. He didn't sound much of a man if his wife could leave him and their daughters and run off to Spain, but he might have a friend, or a brother, or a colleague. You never knew.

In the meantime, she would work on her secondary project, the slimming of Tallulah. Today they were starting the new regime of a long walk in the morning, followed by a few measly dried biscuits for the dog, who was already deeply unimpressed by being denied any snacks or canned food. She had turned her nose up at the dried food last night but Morgan had hardened her heart, remembering Alistair Brown's expression. She wasn't going back to him and admitting that she had failed.

She found some trainers, which were the most practical footwear she had in the absence of Wellington boots, and she and Tallulah set off after breakfast. The sunshine hadn't lasted long and it had turned into another raw day. It was supposed to be spring but there was little sign of it in this part of North Yorkshire and Morgan huddled deeper into her cashmere coat and turned up the collar.

Sadly, Tallulah had less interest in wiping the sneer off Alistair Brown's face and she refused to cooperate with the idea of a brisk walk, sitting down when she was tired, hanging back on the lead and sniffing interminably at any smells she encountered. It was muddy going and Morgan's trainers were soon caked in dirt, which had spattered all the way up to the knees of her extremely expensive designer jeans.

By the time they reached a field which Morgan calculated would take them back on to the narrow lane that led back to Ingleton Hall, she was so fed up with Tallulah's dawdling that she let the dog off the lead and strode off across the downward slope of the field on her own. She would wait for her at the gate at the bottom.

Halfway across the field she stopped and turned to yell at Tallulah to come *on*, but the words died in her throat when, to her horror, she spotted a herd of bullocks lumbering over the crest of the hill and heading towards the oblivious dog who had her nose deep in a grassy clump as she investigated a cowpat.

'Tallulah!' Morgan called sharply, but as Tallulah had never acquired even rudimentary obedience skills she simply ignored Morgan and kept on snuffling.

The bullocks were getting closer. 'Tallulah, come here at *once*!' Morgan's voice rose. Her mother's dog was so stupid the cattle would be on top of her before she had any idea they were there, and then she wouldn't stand a chance. She'd be trampled underfoot.

Morgan might not like Tallulah very much, but she wasn't going to let that happen. She started to run back towards the dog, her heart pounding as the cattle loomed ever closer. Why on earth had she ever thought she wanted to live in the country? At least in London you didn't have to face down a stampede of wild bullocks whenever you went out.

As she and the bullocks converged on Tallulah, Morgan threw a panicky glance over her shoulder. Even if she got to the dog before the bullocks did, what was she going to do with her? The cattle were blocking the way they had come, so she would have to head for the road again, but it seemed a long way away now.

Then she did a double take as she saw two men leaning on the gate.

She waved frantically. 'Help!' she called, but they either didn't hear her or hadn't realised her perilous position. Morgan had no choice but to swoop down on Tallulah, who let out a surprised yelp as she was scooped into the air.

'Go away!' said Morgan more bravely than she felt to the bullocks, who had stopped a few feet away, their flanks heaving as steam billowed from their noses. They were *huge*. 'Shoo!' she tried again, but they didn't move. They just stood there, shifting their hooves ominously.

Oh, God, now what? Tallulah was heavy in her arms, but she didn't dare put her down. She would just have to carry her down to the gate.

She set off, moving very slowly at first in the hope that the bullocks wouldn't notice that she was leaving, but they were still curious about the dog, and followed. The faster Morgan went, the faster they came after her, so that in the end she gave up looking over her shoulder and simply ran as fast as she could down towards the gate.

'Help!' she gasped as she got closer, and at last the two men moved. Closing the gate carefully behind them, they headed to meet her with what seemed an extraordinary lack of haste.

'Oh, thank you, thank you,' Morgan panted as they stepped casually between her and the blundering cattle, who turned away at the waving arms with much blowing and huffing and stamping of hooves, but she was in too much of a panic to stop and help her rescuers and she belted for the safety of the gate and the road beyond.

Too late, she realised that a whole patch of ground in front of the gate had been churned into a sea of mud where the cattle obviously waited for the farmer to arrive with their feed. Before she knew what was happening, she was ankle-deep in mud, her trainers were skidding from beneath her and she was pitching forward. If she hadn't dropped Tallulah and flung out her arms to break her fall, she would have landed splat on her face.

As it was, Tallulah gave an outraged yelp at her undignified landing and floundered desperately towards the gate, ignoring Morgan, who was struggling to keep her balance on her hands and knees in the squelching mud until her hands slipped out and she fell on her face anyway.

For what seemed like an eternity she simply lay there, spread-eagled in the mud, wondering with a detached part of her mind what on earth had happened to sharp, successful, sophisticated Morgan Steele.

Then, very slowly, she hauled herself up to her knees with a disgusting sucking sound, only to realise that there was another, even worse, sound behind her.

Laughter.

The next moment, a hard hand was gripping her elbow and lifting her easily to her feet. Morgan spat out mud and turned to face her rescuer.

It was Alistair Brown.

'I said take the dog for a walk, not train for the hundred metre sprint,' he said, and even in the depths of humiliation Morgan couldn't help noticing how much the broad grin improved his looks. It creased his cheeks, showing strong white teeth, and deepened the fan of lines at the edges of his eyes, banishing that off-putting steeliness and leaving in its stead an alarmingly attractive man.

That was the thing about having goals, Morgan remembered. You needed to define them very carefully. So when she decided to go out and meet attractive men she should have specified that when she achieved her goal she wasn't covered in mud from head to foot.

On the plus side, Alistair wouldn't be able to see the way her cheeks were burning with a potent mixture of exertion and excruciating embarrassment.

'I'm sorry, but that's one of the funniest things I've ever seen,' said Alistair's companion, having shooed the cattle back up the hill. He wiped tears of mirth from his eyes. 'You've never got a camcorder with you when you need one!'

'This is Derek Iverson,' said Alistair to

Morgan, 'and those are his bullocks. We'd just stopped to have a look at them when we saw you belting across here with the dog under your arm! We weren't expecting free entertainment thrown in.'

'I wouldn't have missed it for the world,' said Derek, still chuckling. 'For a slip of a lass, you can certainly move!'

Morgan would have done anything right then to simply disappear but there was nowhere to go but back down into that disgusting mud. She wiped a hand across her mouth but that was muddy too and just made things worse, so she twisted the upper part of her coat sleeve round, about the only piece of her that wasn't covered in mud.

'I'm glad I've provided you with so much amusement,' she said bitterly.

Shaken and still breathless from her panicky run, Morgan was burningly conscious of how ridiculous she must look in her cashmere coat and her designer jeans, smeared in mud from her previously glossy hair to the tips of her ludicrously expensive trainers. She could feel the vet's eyes on her, alight with amusement.

'Are you all right?' he asked belatedly.

'No thanks to you,' she snapped as she looked

for Tallulah, who was huddled against the gate, looking as woebegone as Morgan felt. 'It's lucky my dog and I weren't trampled to death! Those beastly cows are completely wild.'

'That'll teach you to walk across the middle of a field,' he said. 'Don't you know better than that?'

'Funnily enough, we're not taught to evade stampeding wildlife in London!'

'You're not in London now,' he said. 'Next time, check with the farmer first that he doesn't mind you walking on his land, and stick to the edges in case you damage any crops.'

'There won't *be* a next time!' Morgan assured him, realising that her legs were trembling with reaction. 'From now on I'm sticking to tarmac!'

'That won't be much fun for the dog,' Alistair commented.

'What, as opposed to the fun time she's having at the moment? Look at her!' Morgan gestured furiously at Tallulah, miserable and barely recognizable in her mucky brown coating. 'She's absolutely terrified!'

'I'd be terrified too if I'd been happily sniffing a cowpat when some human snatched me up, jolted me down a hillside and threw me in a load of mud!' said Alistair, the corner of his mouth twitching in a way that made Morgan long to hit him. 'You should have let her run on her own. She'd have soon got out of the way of the hooves and it would have been good exercise for her.'

'I think we've had enough exercise for today,' said Morgan. Mustering what little shred of dignity she had, she turned to Derek. 'I'm sorry for walking across your field,' she said stiffly.

'Oh, don't worry about it,' he said jovially. 'You've given me my first laugh of the day! Now that we've met, you can walk here any time.'

'Thank you,' said Morgan, mentally vowing never to set foot in a field again. She fished Talullah's lead out of her pocket and waded awkwardly across the mud to where the dog was still waiting at the gate, tail down and ears drooping. 'Come on, Tallulah, let's go home.'

'I'll give you a lift,' said Alistair, opening the gate for her. In his sturdy rubber boots and overalls, he had no problem negotiating the mud.

'That's really not necessary,' said Morgan through her teeth.

'Don't be silly; you can't walk like that. Look,

the Land Rover's just here. I'm on my way back to the surgery, so I can easily make a detour.'

Pre-empting any further arguments, he took her arm and steered her towards the battered vehicle which was pulled up on the grassy verge in front of a tractor.

'Come on, in you get,' he said. 'And you, Tallulah. No use expecting you to jump, I suppose?'

Bending down, he lifted a startled Tallulah up and deposited her on the floor of the cab before turning to Morgan. 'You know, you might as well give in,' he said, not unkindly.

Suddenly Morgan was close to tears. She would have given anything to have told the heartless Alistair Brown where to stick his lift and to stalk off with her head held high, but her legs were trembling and the mud was cold and revolting and she felt so disgusting that she didn't think she could take another step. And poor Tallulah wasn't in any better shape. Her shaggy paws were clogged with mud and she looked the picture of dejection sitting in the Land Rover. The two of them were a sorry pair.

'All right. Thank you.' she said stiffly, and squelched over to climb in with Tallulah.

Alistair exchanged goodbyes with Derek Iverson and then got in beside her. He glanced at Morgan's set face and then leant across her to open the glove box and pull out a bottle of water.

'Here,' he said, presenting her with the bottle and an old-fashioned white handkerchief he had produced out of his pocket. 'Why don't you clean your face, at least? It'll make you feel better. I've only blown my nose on it twice,' he added as Morgan hesitated and then, seeing her expression change, 'I'm just kidding! It's fresh out of the washing machine this morning and I promise I haven't used it.'

He watched as Morgan used the water to wet the handkerchief and scrub the worst of the muck off her face. Her lips were pressed together in a mixture of disgust and humiliation, but her chin was still lifted at the proud angle he remembered from her visit to the surgery.

'I'm sorry we laughed,' he said, so abruptly that her gaze lifted to his in surprise and he noticed for the first time that she had beautiful eyes the colour of rich dark chocolate.

She stared at him for a moment and then some of the tension left her shoulders and she seemed to slump slightly. 'Oh, it's all right.' She sighed.

'I expect we did look pretty stupid. I seem to spend my whole time at the moment looking or feeling or doing something stupid,' she said fatalistically. 'I should be getting used to it by now.'

'Really?' It was Alistair's turn to be surprised. 'You don't seem like a very stupid person to me,' he said as he started the engine.

'You'd be surprised,' said Morgan, remembering the fibs she had told at the school reunion last year. It had been stupid to let the ghastly Bethany provoke her into inventing a fiancé, that was for sure. Thank God Bethany hadn't had time to ask her any awkward questions about her supposed engagement or it could have ended in a far worse humiliation than falling flat on your face in the mud in front of a laughing vet.

'Appearances can be deceptive,' she told Alistair in a dry voice, and was startled when he glanced at her with a quick smile.

'Quite,' he said, and something about the way his strange, light eyes rested on her sent heat flushing inexplicably through her.

She jerked her gaze from his and turned to look out of the window.

There was a short pause, so short that it hardly

counted as a pause at all, but still Morgan sensed an odd tightening in the air and she was suddenly acutely conscious of the man sitting beside her.

He wasn't spectacular-looking by any means. He had none of Paul's easy glamour and his features were unremarkable except for those piercingly keen eyes that seemed to look right through her.

He was no hunk either, she decided. He was probably a bit taller than her, but not much, and although it was a bit hard to tell under his overalls or the white coat he wore in the surgery, he certainly didn't give the impression of bulging biceps or rippling muscles. Instead, there was a spareness about him, a lean tough-ness that had nothing to do with flaunted muscles but was more about a contained self-assurance that Morgan couldn't help envying.

She might look confident—not now, of course, but in the boardroom she was famously cool and competent—but as soon as she left work behind she reverted to her true existence as a walking, talking mass of seething insecurities. It always amazed Morgan to hear that people found her in-timidating. Couldn't they *see* that she was just as muddled as everyone else?

Alistair's voice jerked her out of her thoughts. 'Where to?'

'To?' echoed Morgan, momentarily disorientated.

'I'll take you home, but I need to know where home is,' he pointed out.

'Oh. Ingleton Hall.'

His brows lifted. 'Ingleton Hall? Really?'

'Do you know it?'

He glanced at her. 'We all know Ingleton Hall. It's famous round here.' Something about his tone riled Morgan.

'You're not going to tell me you believe in ghosts, are you?'

'No.' Alistair paused at the end of the lane before turning right towards Ingleton. 'I was thinking more about the stories about how much has been spent on restoring it. Rumour has it some City whizkid has been throwing silly money at it.'

'It costs a lot of money to restore an old building like the Hall,' said Morgan defensively.

He turned to stare at her as he finally made the connection. '*You're* the whizkid?'

'Well, I don't feel very much of a whiz at the moment,' she said, 'but I certainly bought Ingleton

Hall. Why?' she demanded tartly as he still looked surprised. 'Aren't women allowed to make lots of money and spend it how they like? Is that not how things are done in the country either?'

To her irritation, Alistair seemed more amused than chastened by her sarcasm. 'I guess that explains the pointed boots,' he said, and the corner of his mouth twitched. 'I'm glad to see you're not wearing them today.'

Morgan wanted to snap that she wasn't *stupid*, but right then she didn't think that she could carry it off. The truth was that she felt more than stupid, sitting here covered in mud.

'Of course not,' she muttered instead, with what was intended to be a withering glance that went all wrong as it snagged on the edge of his mouth.

She could see where it curved up at the corner, not quite a smile, but deepening the crease in his cheek and crinkling his eyes intriguingly. It made her remember how he had looked as he'd picked her out of the mud, almost unrecognisable with that broad grin, and for some reason heat fluttered in the pit of her stomach again.

Morgan wrenched her eyes away, only to find them caught by the sight of his hands on the steering wheel instead. They weren't that clean, she couldn't help noticing. She dreaded to think where they had been. If he had been called out to Derek Iverson's farm, chances were that he had been shoulder deep in some cow all morning. Yuk.

Still, if you wanted a pair of hands delivering your calf, Alistair Brown's were probably good ones to have. They were big and square and capable. Morgan watched them resting, sure and steady, on the wheel, and thought about how firm yet gentle they had been as he'd examined Tallulah, in spite of his dismissive attitude.

The memory sent an unexpected shiver down her spine and she turned her head to look out of the passenger window. The view of grey stone walls and green fields was less unsettling.

'So you're the new owner of Ingleton Hall,' Alistair said after a moment. 'How are you enjoying country life?'

'Honestly?' said Morgan, a distinct edge to her voice. 'Not that much right now.' She plucked at her filthy jeans to emphasise the point, but he only grinned.

'You'll feel better when you've had a wash.'

'God, I can't wait. I feel disgusting!'

He shook his head. 'What are you doing in the country if you don't like mud?'

'Right, and I suppose real country people absolutely *love* falling flat on their faces in a pile of mud and cowpats?'

Her withering irony was lost on Alistair. 'You're going to be pretty bored if you're going to avoid mud and fields from now on. What did you think it was going to be like up here?'

'I didn't think about it that much,' Morgan confessed.

Minty would have said that was typical of her. Her twin was always accusing her of being too focused on her goal to think about what she was going to do when she achieved it. 'All you do then is cast around and look for another goal,' Minty had said on more than one occasion.

And that was what she had done with Ingleton Hall, Morgan realised guiltily. It had been a consuming project that had saved her after Paul had left, but she hadn't really thought beyond finishing the restoration and moving in.

'I sold my company,' she told Alistair. 'I wasn't sure what to do with myself when I didn't have to work any more. I wanted to change my life,' she said in a small voice.

It sounded pathetic when she put it like that.

He glanced at the dirty and bedraggled figure beside him. 'It looks as if you've certainly done that.'

'Yes.' A wave of homesickness washed over Morgan as she thought about her old office, sleek and smart and clean. Somebody else would be sitting at her desk now, spinning on her chair to look out over London. Somebody else's mind would be buzzing with the possibility of deals and new ventures instead of feeling the mud and God knew what else drying on their skin and caking under their fingernails.

'Yes,' she said again in a flat voice. 'My life has changed all right.'

She sounded so dejected that Alistair was conscious of a twinge of sympathy.

'What are you going to do with yourself?' he asked.

Morgan remembered the plan she had made that morning. Setting herself another goal, Minty would have said in exasperation. She wondered how Alistair would react if she told him that she was planning to devote her energies to finding a fulfilling relationship.

It would almost be worth the embarrassment to see his face.

Almost, but not quite.

She would have been able to assure him that he wasn't likely to figure on her list of suitable candidates. She wasn't going to get involved with a man who could laugh when you fell on your face. How heartless was that?

He *had* apologised, though.

Anyway, he wasn't her type, Morgan changed tack. He was too brusque, too self-contained. She wanted a man who made her feel wonderful, warm and sexy and desirable. Alistair made her feel like a clumsy idiot. She wanted to be cherished, not criticised, loved, not laughed at.

He could keep his hands and his smile. Morgan believed in setting her sights high, and she wasn't settling for anyone less than perfect this time.

Alistair was looking at her a little oddly and Morgan realised belatedly that she hadn't yet answered his question.

'I'm having a think,' she said. 'I've been asked to join the Board of Governors at the primary school, so maybe that will lead to something.'

Alistair frowned. 'I didn't know that.'

'Why would you?'

'Because I'm a governor myself,' he said. 'I must have missed the meeting when that was discussed. The Chairman's inclined to make snap decisions and inform the Board later.'

He cocked an eyebrow at her. 'That was quick work a week after you've arrived in the village! Why were you invited?'

'In the letter I had, the Chairman said he'd read of my success in the papers,' said Morgan stiffly. 'He seemed to think the Board would profit from having a governor with some business acumen.'

Alistair gave a crack of laughter. 'That sounds like George! He's as pompous as they come.'

'Why were *you* invited?' Morgan retaliated, offended by his dismissive attitude. She had been pleased with the invitation until now.

'My children go to the school.'

'Oh.'

She hadn't had him down as a family man, Morgan had to admit. It was hard to imagine him cuddling a baby or playing with children, let alone falling in love and getting married. He just didn't seem the type somehow.

She wondered what his wife was like. Was she

soft and pretty and adoring? Or sturdy and sensible? Either way, she would be used to his smile, would know how his hands felt, warm and intimate on her skin. She probably didn't think he was cold and brusque at all. She might think of him as loving and passionate.

Morgan swallowed. She felt oddly thrown. There was a sinking feeling in the pit of her stomach which she really, really didn't want to be disappointment. But if it wasn't disappointment, it might be jealousy, and that would be much worse.

Or it could be surprise. Morgan seized on the idea. Yes, that was it. She was just amazed that such a brusque and charmless type had found anyone prepared to marry him, that was all.

Still, she found herself looking forward to the governors' meeting that Thursday more than she had expected. Morgan managed to convince herself it was because of the chance to meet some new people, and she was consequently appalled at how disappointed she was when she discovered that Alistair wasn't there.

Totally unprepared for the strength of her reaction, Morgan was edgy and distracted, and when the Chairman introduced her to the rest of the board and asked her to talk about her experience, her carefully prepared speech went out of her head completely.

She had just recovered her nerve and was getting into her stride when the door opened and Alistair Brown came in with a murmured apology about some veterinary crisis. A pleasant-looking woman with curly hair and an open face made room for him beside her and whispered something as he sat down that made him smile, but he didn't smile at Morgan. He didn't even look at her. He just pulled the agenda towards him and studied it with a slight frown.

His arrival completely threw Morgan. She had been talking so fluently about her knowledge of budgeting and finance, and she longed to impress Alistair for once by talking about her phenomenal success, but suddenly she was stumbling and stuttering and losing her way in the middle of a sentence. It was awful.

'Well, anyway, I hope I'll be able to make a contribution to the village school,' she finished desperately. She had so wanted them all to be pleased and impressed that someone of her experience had chosen to live in their village, but now they would be wondering instead what all the fuss was about.

CHAPTER THREE

IT WAS a relief when they broke for coffee. Morgan was immediately buttonholed by one of the other governors, a tall, good-looking man in his forties who introduced himself as Phil. He was in business himself and delighted to meet her, he said.

Morgan tried to concentrate on what he was saying, but it was hard when over his shoulder she could see Alistair talking to the woman he'd been sitting next to. They didn't seem to be having a very intense conversation, but something about their body language suggested that they were close.

Wrenching her attention back to Phil, Morgan smiled and nodded and reminded herself that he was just the kind of man she had been hoping to meet. She made herself study him objectively. He was certainly attractive, although perhaps not quite as attractive as he thought he was, and not only that, he was available, letting slip early in the conversation that he was divorced. He clearly understood business and was gratifyingly impressed by her. He was flattering too, and gave Morgan the distinct impression that he found her attractive and interesting. What more could she possibly want?

Other than to know what Alistair and that woman were talking about for so long.

Morgan was glad when George joined them and she was able to steer the conversation round to the other governors. 'I've met Alistair Brown,' she said casually. 'Is that his wife he's talking to?'

George and Phil looked across at Alistair and his companion. 'No, that's Cathy Reid,' said Phil. 'Nice woman. No one can understand how her husband could have left her.'

'He must need his head examined,' George agreed. 'You'd be hard pushed to find a kinder person. She's struggling to bring up two boys on her own, but she still has time to volunteer for all sorts of things in the village. She's a wonderful, cook, too,' he went on fondly. 'Her cakes are always the first to go at the summer fete.'

Morgan didn't really want to know how marvellous Cathy Reid was. She was more interested in finding out about Alistair's wife, but she couldn't think of a way to ask without seeming nosy.

Cathy might not be Alistair's wife, but she was certainly very comfortable with him, Morgan thought acidly, watching the other woman laugh up at him. She had a heart-shaped face, a mass of curly hair and a generously curved figure that stopped just short of being plump.

In fact, Morgan realised uncomfortably, Cathy was the exact opposite of her. Nobody would ever call Cathy intimidating. She was fair and cosy, while Morgan was dark and striking, and she looked sensible rather than clever. Morgan was prepared to bet that Cathy would never run squealing from a few cows, or fall on her face in the mud.

Watching her, Morgan suddenly felt depressed. She was all wrong here. She had tried to dress down, knowing that it would be inappropriate to look too smart, and she had thought her black trousers and silk cardigan would be casual enough to seem as if she hadn't made a particular effort. But next to the simple jeans and faded shirt that Cathy was wearing she knew that she looked far too elegant and expensive to ever belong in this simple village primary school.

George was making noises about returning to the meeting and there was a general movement towards the door. Morgan found herself next to Alistair and Cathy.

'You're looking a bit cleaner than when I last saw you,' he said.

Uncomfortably aware of his lean, taut body beside hers, Morgan smiled tightly. 'I'm still finding mud in places I shouldn't.'

Remembering his manners, Alistair introduced Cathy. 'Morgan—it is Morgan, isn't it?—had an unfortunate encounter with Derek Iverson's bullocks the other day,' he told Cathy.

Morgan was furious at the way he had hesitated over her name. She hadn't had any trouble remembering *his* name. He obviously hadn't given her a moment's thought since dropping her off that day, and she wished passionately that she could say the same.

'Oh, dear,' said Cathy. 'Bullocks can be very nasty. You didn't hurt yourself, did you?'

'Just my pride,' said Morgan, perversely annoyed that Cathy was being friendly and sympathetic instead of sneering at her for being such a city girl.

'I'm so impressed by what you've managed to achieve,' Cathy went on. 'I would never have had the guts to build a company from scratch and take the risks you did! I was just saying to Alistair what an incredible person you must be.'

Morgan glanced at Alistair. As she expected, he was looking faintly derisive, and she put up her chin. 'And what did Alistair say?' she challenged him.

Alistair's face was perfectly straight, but the cool grey eyes held an unmistakable glint of amusement. 'I said she can run fast, too,' he said.

Morgan consulted the map the twins had drawn for her, then turned it round and studied it upside down. She glanced to her right. If the church was *there* and the pub over *there*, this must be their house.

It was a typical Yorkshire village house, built in grey stone, square and sturdy and unpretentious. Morgan felt surprisingly nervous as she pushed open the wooden gate and walked up to knock on the front door. She hoped the twins had been right when they'd told her that their father was looking forward to meeting her. After her encounters with Alistair Brown her confidence was drooping somewhere in the vicinity of her ankles. It would be nice to meet someone quiet and inoffensive who didn't make her feel the size of a gnat.

Polly and Phoebe had been back to visit her the day before, bearing what they'd assured her was an invitation from their father for tea. They had come with her to walk Tallulah, chattering all the way, and then had a wonderful time in the pool while Morgan watched anxiously. Children made her nervous. They were always doing something alarming. She wished that they would just sit still sometimes, but the twins had made the most of having such a wonderful pool all to themselves and they'd splashed up and down, telling Morgan about their life.

'Mum lives in Spain. She's got a boyfriend called Jaime, but we don't like him very much,' Phoebe said. 'He's got a house with a pool too, but it's outside and it's not nearly as nice as this.'

'How often do you see your mother?' Morgan hoped she wasn't being too nosy, but the twins didn't seem to mind.

'We go out in the holidays. It's OK, but we prefer living with Dad, even if he is a bit cross sometimes.'

'He's brought you up on his own, has he?'

They nodded. 'Since we were six,' said Polly.

'It can't have been easy for him.'

'He cut off our hair,' said Phoebe. 'He said he didn't have time to do pretty plaits like Mum used to do, so we're not allowed to have long hair any more.'

Poor little mites, thought Morgan. Abandoned by their mother and left with a father who couldn't be bothered with feminine trifles. Still, she had to admit that they didn't seem too traumatised. She had rarely met such confident and self-possessed children.

Morgan wasn't sure what was the appropriate attire when you were invited out for tea, but she was fairly sure she was going to look overdressed whatever she wore. She just didn't possess anything faded or scruffy. In the end she had opted for a soft skirt with a silk jumper in her favourite neutral colours and a chunky leather belt slung around her hips.

Readjusting the belt now, she lifted a hand to knock on the door.

Barely half an hour earlier, Alistair had got in after an emergency call out to a dog that had a ball stuck in its throat. He had managed to save it, but it had been touch and go. He had put the kettle on, hoping to settle down for a quiet time with the paper and a mug of tea. His daughters, however, had other ideas, and were pestering him to go and get changed while they bickered over how to make scones.

'There's a packet of biscuits in the tin,' he told them absently as he unfolded the sports section. 'We don't need scones.'

'We want to make a nice tea. Dad, can't you at least change your shirt? It's all torn.'

'A rip here or there isn't going to change the taste of the scones,' he pointed out without looking up from the paper.

'Oh, *please*, Dad,' they pleaded with him, then jumped as the dogs went into a frenzy of barking at the sound of a knock on the door.

The girls exchanged an excited look. 'You go,' Polly said to her sister, who hesitated then followed the dogs to the door.

Alistair frowned. 'What's going on?'

'We've invited someone for tea,' said Polly with an edge of defiance. 'She's nice. We thought you'd like to meet her.'

Alistair's heart sank. He didn't feel like

meeting anyone right now, let alone some woman the twins had picked out for him, but clearly it was too late to do anything about it.

He heard the murmur of voices interspersed with excited barks, and turned to see Morgan, bending to pat Tip, the Labrador cross he had rescued, and trying to squeeze past him into the kitchen at the same time. As she straightened, though, she caught sight of Alistair sitting at the kitchen table and her expression of appalled recognition was probably a fairly accurate mirror of his own, Alistair thought.

'Oh,' she said, stopping dead so that Phoebe cannoned into her. 'It's you.'

For a moment she looked as if she would really like to turn tail and run, then her chin lifted in a gesture that Alistair remembered. 'Hello.'

'Hello.'

Alistair put down his paper and got to his feet, startled by how familiar she seemed standing there, a wary expression in the beautiful dark eyes. He hadn't taken to Morgan when he had first met her in the surgery. She had seemed brittle and spoilt and he'd doubted that she would last the winter here. Her panicky reaction to a few bullocks had just underscored that, but he had to admit to a grudging respect for the way she had picked herself out of the mud. He really wished that he hadn't laughed at her, funny as the sight had been.

Then the other night, at the governors' meeting, she had seemed cool and aloof and out of place once more. Alistair couldn't think why Cathy should be so impressed by her. As far as he could see, Morgan had just been wearing trousers and a cardigan, but Cathy had sighed enviously over what she'd called Morgan's stylishness.

Privately, Alistair had decided that Morgan was just a little too clever for her own good. Too much about her reminded him of Shelley. That single-mindedness, the ruthless pursuit of what they wanted, regardless of who got in their way, the disdain for those of them that didn't need smart cars or fancy clothes to be happy. No, Morgan was a type and he didn't like it.

Still, there was something about her that stuck in his mind and he hadn't quite been able to shake the memory of the snap in those chocolate-brown eyes, that combative lift of her chin, the grittiness of her expression as she had wiped mud from her face.

And now here she was in his kitchen, looking

down her nose and clearly no more pleased to see him than he was to see her.

There was an awkward silence, then Alistair moved forward. For whatever reason, Polly and Phoebe had decided that they liked her, so he would have to make the best of it. 'Come in,' he said. 'You must be the reason for the scones. I didn't know the girls had met you.'

'They told me that you'd invited me,' she said, and they both turned to look at the twins.

'We knew you wouldn't mind,' said Phoebe brazenly. 'You don't, do you, Dad?'

Actually he did mind, as he would point out in no uncertain terms later, but he could hardly say so now. 'Of course not,' he said.

It was clear to Morgan that the last thing he wanted to do was to entertain anyone. He was wearing jeans and a grey T-shirt beneath a scruffy checked shirt and his feet were bare, but he had an assurance that counted for far more than any smart suit. Morgan wished that she looked as comfortable and at ease with her own body, but something about him immediately made her feel stiff and awkward.

'Look, perhaps I'd better go,' she began.

Something in her expression made Alistair

put out a hand to stop her. Perhaps, he thought with compunction, she wasn't quite as tough as she appeared.

'Please don't,' he said. 'The girls will be disappointed.'

'Yes, don't go, Morgan,' they said. 'We've made you scones specially.'

'There you go. How can you resist their scones?' said Alistair as Morgan still hesitated. 'It's a lovely afternoon. We'll go and sit in the garden and Polly and Phoebe can bring us tea since this is their surprise.'

Morgan felt awkward. She could hardly insist on going now. It would just hurt the girls' feelings, as he had said. She would just have a quick cup of tea and then go, she decided.

Alistair showed her out on to a small terrace that was sheltered from the brisk wind, and in the weak sun it was quite pleasant to sit and look out over a garden as plain and unpretentious as the house to the purple moors that rolled away in the distance. The two dogs bustled out too, not wanting to be left out of the action.

'You didn't bring the dog with you?' said Alistair, sitting down next to Morgan on the old wooden bench.

'No.' Morgan was very conscious of him beside her. It wasn't that big a bench, but there hadn't been anywhere else to sit. His closeness made her suddenly aware of the beat of her heart and the tingle of something disturbing beneath her skin. 'She's already had two walks today and she's exhausted.'

'Are you sticking to the diet, too?'

'Yes, but it's not easy,' said Morgan. 'She's got her early Christian martyr act off to perfection now. When she finds out that I've just put that dried food in her bowl instead of biscuits, she looks at me as if I've kicked her, then puts her tail down and trails off, and I feel *awful*! I notice she goes back and eats it later, though.'

To her surprise, Alistair laughed. 'These two are the same,' he said, nodding at the dogs. Tip was wiping his face on the lawn, while the wire-haired Jack Russell, called Bert, was worrying a ball. 'They know just how to pluck at the heart-strings when they want something, usually food. They're like children. They seem to have an inbuilt capacity for emotional blackmail!'

The mention of children made Morgan wonder why Phoebe and Polly had gone to such lengths to get her here, and she remembered her initial suspicion that they might be matchmaking. The very thought made her go cold with embarrassment. They could hardly have got it more wrong!

'I didn't realise you were Polly and Phoebe's father,' she said awkwardly, just in case he thought she had any hand in the plot, if that was what it was. 'I thought you were married.'

'No, not for the last five years anyway,' said Alistair in a dry voice. 'Did the girls tell you?'

'They said their mother lived in Spain.'

He nodded. 'Shelley always hated the country life. She was bored, and she complained constantly that I was never there. She didn't seem to understand that a vet can't just drop everything and go home at five o'clock every day. She found the twins hard work as babies too, and she never really got into the village community where she'd have met other mothers.'

Leaning forward, Alistair rested his forearms on his knees and watched the two dogs who were now wrestling amiably on the lawn. 'She told me one day that she'd been taking a long hard look at her life and decided that she wanted something more exciting, so she was going off to "find herself" in Spain. I don't know if she ever found herself,' he went on, an ironic twist to his mouth, 'but she found Jaime, and she's been there ever since.'

'But…how could she leave her children?' asked Morgan.

Alistair shrugged. 'You'd have to ask her that. She couldn't take them with her at first in any case. She was living with Jaime, who hadn't yet broached the subject of divorce with his wife, and they didn't have much room. Besides, she would have needed my permission to take the girls out of the country and there was no way I was going to let them go off to Spain where I wouldn't be able to see them.'

'I'm sorry,' said Morgan quietly after a moment. 'It must have been very difficult for you.'

Alistair sighed and sat up once more. 'Let's just say I wouldn't recommend bringing up children on your own as a soft option.'

'Polly and Phoebe seem very…well-adjusted,' said Morgan, and he smiled at her careful choice of adjective.

'They're little minxes,' he said roundly. 'I hope they haven't been making a nuisance of themselves?'

'No, no,' she said hastily. 'They're good company.'

'How did you meet them, anyway?'

'They came to interview me for the school magazine.'

'What school magazine?' asked Alistair.

They looked at each other. Morgan's heart sank at the dawning suspicion in his eyes. She had a nasty feeling that he was coming to the same conclusions that she had.

'What are those two up to?' he said ominously after a moment. 'They'd better not be match-making again!'

'Again?' Morgan hadn't been expecting that.

Alistair shook his head ruefully. 'They tried to find me a girlfriend a couple of years ago. They'd got it into their heads that I should get married again and latched on to their teacher, who happened to be single. They kept asking me if I liked her and could they ask her round… It was all very awkward! It was a huge relief when the poor girl married someone else and moved away.'

At least he didn't suspect her of having designs on him, Morgan reassured herself. It would have been mortifying if he'd assumed that she had somehow set this meeting up herself, but clearly he was used to his daughters' machinations.

'*Have* you ever thought about marrying again?' she asked him.

His mouth turned down at the corners. 'I know it would make things easier in lots of ways if I did,' he said, 'but my first marriage wasn't the kind that made me keen to rush out and repeat the experience. Practically, it would solve a lot of problems if I had a wife—it would save a lot of money on childcare, for a start! At the moment I have to pay for an au pair to be here just in case I'm called out at night, but they never stay long. There's not enough for them to do in the village. At the moment we've got Bodil, and she can't wait to get away to Leeds or York at the weekend.'

'It sounds as if you want a wife to be a kind of glorified housekeeper,' said Morgan disapprovingly. 'Why don't you just employ a proper housekeeper instead of all these young girls who are obviously going to be bored and lonely here?'

'I would if I could afford it, but I can't,' said Alistair. 'In any case, I don't need a housekeeper. I'm more than capable of running the house myself. I just need someone to be here with the twins when I'm on call at night.

'Anyway, that's all beside the point,' he went on. 'I don't see any likelihood of me getting married in the near future. I'd certainly consider it if I could find someone suitable, but Polly and Phoebe never like any of my girlfriends, and I never like any of the women they think would be good for me.'

Alistair stopped abruptly, realising too late the implications of what he had said. 'Of course, I don't mean *you*…' he said awkwardly.

'Of *course* not,' said Morgan, rather enjoying his discomfiture—let him feel what it was like for a change!—and therefore making no effort to conceal her sarcasm.

They were interrupted just then by Polly, staggering out with a laden tea tray, which she plonked on the wooden table by the bench, and Phoebe, who had clearly been deputed to bring chairs for the two of them. These she arranged carefully so that they could observe how their father and Morgan were getting on while Polly laboriously poured out the tea.

The scones were burnt and practically inedible, but Morgan chewed manfully on one and pronounced it delicious.

'They're a bit hard,' said Polly, disappointed, and then she brightened. 'Maybe you could help us make them next time?'

'I'm afraid I don't know anything about baking,' she said. 'I've never even tried to make a cake.'

The girls were momentarily daunted. 'Well, we could learn together, then,' Phoebe suggested. 'It would be fun.'

'Morgan might not want to learn how to bake,' Alistair interrupted. He set his mug on the arm of the bench and eyed his daughters sternly. 'Now, what's all this about, you two?'

'Nothing,' they said, identical eyes wide, the picture of innocence.

Alistair wasn't fooled. He had seen them look like that before. He waited patiently, without taking his penetrating gaze off them, until they began to fidget.

'We saw this programme,' Polly burst out at last.

'It was reality TV,' Phoebe added, 'and you had these children choosing a partner for their mum or dad.'

Alistair pressed the fingers of one hand against his temples. 'God, what will they think of next?' he muttered.

'But it was really good, Dad,' Polly tried to explain. 'They reckoned the children were much better at knowing what the parents needed. They gave them all interviews—that's the single people—and then they picked the one they thought would be best, and then the mum or the dad went out on a date, and they all said they *really* liked the person their kids had chosen.'

'So we thought we could do that for you. We emailed the programme to see if we could take part, but they said they weren't doing another series,' said Phoebe regretfully, unaware of her father blenching at the prospect of his children matchmaking in front of an audience of millions.

'And then we read about Morgan in the paper and we thought she sounded really cool. It said she wasn't married, so we decided to do our own interview.'

'So it wasn't for the school magazine at all?' said Morgan.

'No, but we had to say that because you'd think it was funny if we said we wanted to interview you to see if you'd get on with our dad. And we think you *would*,' Polly assured her.

'It would be so cool if we could come and live with you,' Phoebe hurried on, before Morgan had a chance to say anything. 'I'm sure you must be lonely in that house by yourself, so we could be like a ready-made family for you. It would be better for everybody. Dad wouldn't worry about money so much so he wouldn't be so grumpy, and I could have a computer in a room of my own, and Polly could have a pony, and we could go on holiday,' she finished breathlessly, quite carried away at the thought of the glorious future that could be theirs.

'We never go on holiday,' Polly added.

'You go to Spain three times a year,' said Alistair, tight-jawed. He hardly dared look at Morgan to see how she was taking this revelation of quite how ruthlessly materialistic his daughters were.

'That's to visit Mum,' said Phoebe dismissively. 'A holiday's different. We could go to America! Annie and Luke went last year and they said it was great!'

'*And* you could get a decent car, instead of driving around in that dirty old thing you've got now,' Polly pointed out. 'It's so shaming!'

'I think that's enough,' said Alistair sharply. More than enough. 'I'm not marrying Morgan just to get a new car, and she deserves better than being used as a passport to New York! You ought to be ashamed of yourselves. How do you think Morgan feels to know that you're only interested in her because she's rich?'

Both girls looked dismayed at the idea. 'But we really like you, too,' Polly tried to explain and Phoebe nodded vigorously.

'You don't talk to us like we're little children, the way Cathy does. She's always trying to *help* us, and she fusses. You don't fuss. We think you'd be a really good stepmother.'

'And you did *say* you wouldn't mind stepchildren,' Polly reminded Morgan, who flushed.

'I was talking generally,' she said. 'I didn't think you'd take it as the go-ahead to fix me up on a blind date with your father!'

'Quite,' said Alistair, and turned back to Polly and Phoebe, who were looking distinctly mutinous. 'Did you hear what Morgan said? Now, you've both got to stop this matchmaking nonsense right now! I want you to apologise to Morgan for putting her in an extremely awkward situation.'

'But, Dad...'

'*Now*,' he said.

The girls subsided. 'Sorry, Morgan,' they muttered.

'That's OK,' said Morgan, feeling nearly as uncomfortable as they did now. 'There's no harm done.'

'Perhaps not, but they've got to realise that they can't try and manipulate people like that.' Alistair regarded his daughters under lowered brows. 'You might think you're grown up, but you're not. You're just children, and you don't understand that adult relationships are tricky.

'It's not just a question of looking for the right bank balance,' he went on, feeling his way cautiously as he tried to make them understand. 'You want to find someone you like as a friend and find attractive, and there has to be a kind of spark between you that you can't explain. That's the most important thing you can have in a relationship, and if it isn't there, there's nothing you can do about it.

'There's no spark between Morgan and me,' he told them. 'She doesn't find me attractive, and she doesn't want to marry me. Do you, Morgan?' he asked suddenly, turning to her for reinforcement.

For a moment, Morgan played with the idea of saying that yes, actually, she did, just to see what he would say. It wasn't as if he had left her much choice, she thought crossly. She could hardly turn round and assure him that *she* had felt a spark, could she?

Not that she had, Morgan told herself hastily.

She just didn't like being put in a position where she couldn't speak for herself.

However, in this case, there was nothing else she *could* say, even if she had wanted to. 'Of course not,' she said.

'And I don't find Morgan attractive and I don't want to marry her either,' Alistair informed his daughters.

Charming, thought Morgan sourly. Just what her ego needed.

'So you girls are just going to have to forget all these plans you've made,' he was saying. 'I know you want ponies and computers and trips to New York, but there are ways to get what you want without involving anyone else. You need to learn to work for what you want, rather than just hoping that you'll acquire a wealthy stepmother! You're not to do this again. Do you understand?'

Polly and Phoebe looked at each other. It was clear to Morgan that they disagreed with their father, but they weren't prepared to defy him outright.

'Yes, Dad,' they muttered.

Alistair sent them off with the tray to clear up the tea things, then raked a hand through his hair. 'I'm sorry about that,' he said to Morgan.

'It's OK,' she said, trying not to remember how definite he had been about not finding her attractive 'They were just thinking about you.'

'And themselves, materialistic little so-and-sos!'

'They wouldn't be the first children to put their own interests first,' Morgan commented, wishing that she wasn't so aware of him sitting so close beside her.

She was trying hard to keep her eyes fixed on the garden, but he kept snagging at the edge of her vision. He was lounging back on the bench, legs stretched out ahead of him, bare feet crossed at the ankle. She could see the fine hairs at his wrist, the firm line of his jaw, the way his brow drew together as he watched the dogs with a preoccupied frown. It was clear that he wasn't aware of her at all. He might as well have been sitting next to a sack of potatoes or one of his dogs.

No, not a dog. He would pay a dog more attention. He might put a hand on its head or fondle its ears absently.

Lucky dog.

Morgan was horrified as the thought slipped into her mind before she had a chance to see it coming and stop it in its tracks. She pushed it firmly away and made herself concentrate fiercely on the view.

'You think if you bring children up in a village like this they'll grow up appreciating the country, all the space and freedom that they have,' Alistair was saying, oblivious to the wayward trend of Morgan's thoughts, 'but of course they just take it all for granted. They watch television just like city children watch television. They use the Internet. They know exactly what brand of trainers they should be wearing, what kind of mobile phone they should have, which computer games are cool…'

He sighed and leant forward again to rest his arms on his thighs. 'They're all at it. Their friends get taken on skiing trips or off to New York and of course they want those things too. I don't know how other parents afford it, to be honest. I'm not exactly on the breadline, but by the time I've paid for the mortgage and childcare and sending them to see their mother three times a year, I can't afford to buy Polly a pony or Phoebe her own computer, and it's no use pretending that I can.'

'It won't kill them to grow up without them,' said Morgan, sensing that what depressed him was not so much the lack of cash but the feeling that he had somehow failed his daughters. 'They're not exactly deprived.'

'No, but…' Alistair trailed off.

'But what?'

He hesitated for a moment. 'Shelley's boyfriend, Jaime, runs several hotels in Spain,' he confided in a burst. 'He always seems to have plenty of money. Right now the girls aren't that impressed by him but as they get older…well, I guess I'm afraid they might begin to see the advantages of going to live with their mother. Shelley's always dropping hints about how she can offer them a better life than me.'

'But it's you they choose to live with,' Morgan pointed out. 'Yes, they like the idea of ponies and pools and computers, but they know what's most important to them, and that's you.'

CHAPTER FOUR

CONSCIOUS of a slight lightening of the heart, Alistair turned his head to look up at Morgan from where he was leaning on his knees. He was surprised that he had told her so much. She was practically a stranger, after all, but she was a good listener. You didn't feel that she would offer platitudes or pity or make silly suggestions. She just listened carefully and made comments that were cool and sensible but more helpful than any amount of sympathy.

He studied her with new interest. She had probably never been pretty, he thought, but she had clearly grown into her looks. She had the kind of strong, intelligent face that could look plain on a young girl but suited an older woman. It was full of character, and her eyes were particularly beautiful. He was surprised that he hadn't noticed quite how remarkable they were before.

She had a generously curved mouth too, and it occurred to Alistair that he had never seen her smile, not properly. She looked as if she was someone who would throw her head back and laugh given half a chance, and he was sorry that he hadn't seen it for himself.

Perhaps she hadn't had a lot to laugh about, he thought with compunction.

She certainly wasn't laughing now. She was probably bored stiff, listening to his domestic problems. What did she care, after all?

'I shouldn't be boring you with all this, anyway,' he said, recollecting himself as he straightened. 'It's not your problem.'

Which sounded to Morgan as if he was regretting confiding in her. 'I should be going,' she said, and got to her feet.

Alistair stood up as well. 'Look, I'm sorry about the girls putting you in such an awkward situation. I hope it wasn't embarrassing for you.'

'You don't get to run your own company if you're easily embarrassed,' said Morgan. 'Don't worry about it. At least they were honest, and there's a lot to be said for that. I think we can all safely say we know where we stand now!'

'You've been very nice about it,' said Alistair,

thinking how much more approachable she seemed all of a sudden. He had always had the impression that she was looking down her nose at everyone before, but she had been very understanding about the twins and he felt bad now that he hadn't been friendlier.

There was no sign of Polly and Phoebe as he walked Morgan back to the front door. 'Thank the girls for tea,' she said, and Alistair appreciated the ironic edge to her voice.

'Come again,' he said impulsively. 'Now we know that neither of us is interested in a relationship, there's no reason we shouldn't all be friends, is there? The girls really do like you, you know. They'd be sorry not to see you again.'

'There's no question of that,' said Morgan. 'I like them, too. They're welcome to come and see me whenever they like. As they pointed out, I've got a lovely pool and no one to swim in it.'

'That's kind of you,' he said, meaning it. 'They'd like that.'

There was a tiny pause.

It was all very well for Alistair to suggest that they were all friends, thought Morgan, but he didn't seem the kind of friend she could kiss on the cheek or hug goodbye, and you didn't shake hands if you were friends, did you?

'Well…goodbye, then,' she said with a bright smile.

'Goodbye, Morgan,' he said, lifting a hand in farewell. 'And thanks again.'

Morgan wasn't sure how she felt as she walked home. Better, she thought. Against all expectations, it seemed that Alistair might turn out to be a friend after all, which was good. of course.

So he didn't find her attractive? That was just as well, Morgan tried to convince herself. She wasn't attracted to him either.

It was just that she couldn't get the image of his mouth off her mind. She could picture him with uncomfortable clarity as he had sat there on the bench next to her. The cool face with those keen grey eyes. The square capable hands. The easy way he inhabited his scruffy clothes. The gleam of humour that warmed his expression and the dry exasperation that entirely failed to conceal the depth of his love for his daughters.

Really, it was just as well they had got the whole relationship thing out of the way, Morgan decided. Alistair's announcement that he didn't find her attractive might have been a bit brutal, but at least it was honest and there were no grounds for misunderstandings. She could carry on with her search to find a man who *did* find her attractive and she and Alistair could be friends without any complications or awkwardness. Perfect.

Funny how the thought didn't cheer her up, though.

The Hall felt empty when she got home. Morgan was surprised at how pleased she was to see Tallulah, who waddled to greet her with a wheezy bark. She wasn't quite alone.

As she cooked herself a lonely supper, which she wasn't even allowed to share with Tallulah because of her strict diet, Morgan couldn't help imagining how different things would be if Phoebe and Polly's plans had borne fruit. The house wouldn't feel empty with two eleven-year-old girls, three dogs (because presumably Tip and Bert would move in too) and Alistair.

Alistair. He would sit at the kitchen table and chat to the girls while Morgan cooked, and every now and then she would meet his eyes and they would smile. Or perhaps the girls wouldn't be there at all? Perhaps they were in the pool, so that she and Alistair were snatching a few moments alone. He might catch hold of her waist and pull her down on to his knee, he might tell her to forget the cooking and kiss him instead, he might hold her hard against him and press his lips against her throat and whisper that he couldn't wait until later when he could take her to bed and make love to her...

All the breath was sucked out of Morgan at the thought, and for a moment she felt quite dizzy. She could imagine it all with alarming—no, *terrifying*—clarity. The warmth of his lips. The sureness of his hands. The hardness of his body. The curve of his smile against her skin.

Morgan swallowed hard, realised that she had forgotten to take a breath and gulped a lungful of air. Something warm and dangerous was prowling around the base of her spine and her stomach clenched with a little shiver. She felt disturbed and disorientated, even faintly sick, as if she had been jolted out of a pleasant dream.

And that was when the phone rang.

Afterwards, Morgan often wondered how differently her life would have turned out if she had just left it. She so nearly didn't pick it up, but she had wondered if Minty had realised in the way twins did that she was feeling restless and uneasy and had rung to see if she was all right. They had often called each other at critical times, just knowing somehow that things weren't quite right for the other one.

But when Morgan answered the phone it wasn't Minty at all.

'Hi, Morgan,' said a voice that most definitely did not belong to her twin. 'It's Bethany here.'

For a moment, Morgan was so thrown at it not being Minty that she couldn't say anything. She held the phone away from her ear and stared at it. This couldn't be happening. Please, please, *please*, let her not have said Bethany!

'Bethany Harrington-French... Bethany Simmons as was. You remember, we met again at the school reunion in October.'

Oh, God, it *was* Bethany! Morgan's heart, having already taken a bit of battering that evening as it was, plummeted to her feet. Just thinking about the things she had said last time she met Bethany was enough to make her cringe with embarrassment.

'Oh...yes, of course...hello, Bethany,' she said, wondering how on earth Bethany had tracked her down. She thought she had made a point of not giving her a card.

'Minty gave me your number,' said Bethany as

if reading her mind. 'We had a nice chat. My lot are about the same age as hers—you know what we mums are like when we get together!'

She gave the tinkling laugh that never failed to set Morgan's teeth on edge. Even at fifteen there had been a smugness about Bethany which the intervening years had only intensified. Most of the women Morgan knew had had their confidence dented by life in one way or another, but not Bethany. She just carried on being the prettiest girl in the school who had married a wealthy bank executive, and whose three angelic children and membership of the tennis club and a marvellous dinner party set had armoured her in complacency.

What Morgan hated most about her, though, was the effortless way Bethany was able to make her feel fifteen again, gawky and plain and unpopular. Not that Bethany was ever unpleasant. That wouldn't have bothered Morgan. No, it was the sickly sweetness that Morgan couldn't stand, the syrupy way Bethany tried to 'help'. She was always full of suggestions as to how Morgan could improve her looks, or make more friends, all of which might have gone down better if they hadn't been accompanied by a little sting in the tail.

'You know, Morgan, if you learnt how to make

up your eyes, it would draw attention away from your nose,' Bethany would say sweetly. Or, 'I've got a new cleanser that's really good for spots. You can have it if you like. I don't really need it any more.' Or, 'Looks aren't everything, Morgan. You shouldn't be so sensitive. Beauty's only skin-deep.'

Ah, yes, Morgan had loved that one.

'What can I do for you, Bethany?' she asked.

It turned out that Bethany wanted to bring her entire family to stay with Morgan. 'I read about your fabulous house in one of those design magazines, and I said to Hugh, we *must* go and see it. I hadn't realised you were quite that successful, Morgan,' she added with a hint of reproach. 'You didn't say anything about having your own company at the reunion.'

That's because you were too busy talking about your marvellous husband and your marvellous kids and your marvellous life and making me feel inadequate for not having any of them, Morgan thought.

There was a certain irony in the fact that Bethany was now courting her, Morgan reflected. She knew why, of course. In her own way, she was famous, or at least in business circles. Sometimes there were articles about her in the women's pages, all of which stressed her success and her singleness. She was constantly being asked to explain why she wasn't married, as if her commercial success was somehow devalued because she wasn't equally successful in the emotional stakes. To be *really* successful, it seemed, you had to have a husband and children to show off along with your flourishing company and stellar bank balance.

Bethany wouldn't waste much time on the business pages, but she was an avid devotee of magazines devoted to the home and garden. She would have been impressed to have seen Morgan's house featured there, and the accompanying article had noted her spectacular business career, although it hadn't made any mention of her private life. It was the only reason Morgan had agreed to the article in the first place, but she was so proud of Ingleton Hall, she hadn't been able to resist the chance to show it off.

Now she wished she hadn't. Bethany had read it and decided that she was some kind of mini celebrity, and she would never leave her alone now. The woman was a relentless social climber and Morgan would now be seen as someone she could produce at a dinner party.

Or…no, she wasn't dinner party material, Morgan realised, thinking about it. Bethany would only entertain couples. But she would probably be someone Bethany could boast about, especially if she could say that she had stayed in what the magazine had called her 'lovely home'.

Somehow Morgan was going to have to head this one off.

'Of course it would be lovely to see you, Bethany,' she said. 'But I am quite busy at the moment. When were you thinking of coming?'

Because I will definitely be busy, whenever it is.

'Oh, we're completely flexible,' said Bethany airily. 'We can come whenever it suits you.'

Morgan chewed her thumb. How was she going to get out of this now? She was tempted to say that she was busy for the rest of her life, but Bethany had the hide of a rhinoceros and would just keep pushing until Morgan agreed.

'Well, it's a bit awkward,' she temporised, trying to think of an excuse.

Why was she so pathetic when it came to Bethany? The woman had no power over her now. She was silly and patronising and Morgan had never liked her, but she still had the ability to reduce Morgan's confidence to shreds and make her feel like the ugly, awkward girl she had been when Bethany was in her prime.

'Awkward? Oh…oh, I *see*,' said Bethany, oozing sympathy. 'Didn't things work out with your chap? You haven't had much luck with relationships, have you?'

'It's nothing like that,' spluttered Morgan, furious at the immediate assumption Bethany had made, correct though it was. 'Everything's fine,' she lied.

'You're still getting married?'

Morgan's fingers clenched on the phone. See how much trouble two glasses of wine can get you in? she asked herself bitterly. If only she hadn't opened her big mouth at that ghastly reunion, but Bethany had been so condescending about the fact that, at thirty-nine, Morgan had no husband and children to bore people about that she had been quite unable to resist the temptation of wiping that pitying smile off her face.

And she couldn't go back on it now. Bethany would just see that as proof of how sad Morgan was. Imagine, she would tell people confidingly, poor old Morgan was so desperate that she was actually reduced to *inventing* a fiancé!

Morgan could hear the little laugh that would accompany that juicy bit of gossip even now. No, there was no way she was coming clean now!

'We haven't fixed a date for the wedding yet, but we're very much in love,' she told Bethany defiantly.

'Oh, super. What's his name?' asked Bethany. 'I don't think I caught it last time.'

No, that was because she had been careful to end the conversation before Bethany had time to demand any more details.

Now Morgan cast frantically around for inspiration, and for some reason Alistair Brown's face popped into her mind.

'Alistair,' she said with something of a gasp, crossing her fingers and reasoning that he would never know. 'Alistair Brown.'

'What does he do?' Always an important question for the Bethanys of this world.

'He's a vet.' Oh, to hell with it! In for a penny, in for a pound, thought Morgan. She might as well appropriate Alistair's entire life. At least that way she could keep her lies consistent. 'He's divorced and has twin daughters.'

'Oh, a ready-made family for you? How sweet!'

There was just the slightest edge to Bethany's voice and Morgan had the distinct impression that she would have preferred it if Morgan had admitted to another failed relationship. The possibilities for patronising her then would have been endless.

'We'll look forward to meeting them all,' Bethany continued. 'My lot will be company for Alistair's girls, and they can keep each other amused while we have a lovely catch up on all the gossip. Now, what about the seventh of May? Or we can make it another day if that doesn't suit you.'

She would, too, Morgan realised. Bethany would just keep on rearranging until she got what she wanted. She might as well give in now.

'The seventh sounds fine,' she said, desperate to get Bethany off the phone.

It seemed a lifetime before Bethany finally said goodbye and hung up, leaving Morgan to sink into a chair and drop her head on to the kitchen table.

God, what had she done? And how on earth was she going to get out of it now?

In a panic Morgan rang Minty, who took a very casual view of the whole thing, as she could afford to do, not having to face the prospect of twenty-four hours in Bethany's company.

'She's ghastly, isn't she?' she was all she would say. 'I'm glad *I* don't have a fabulous house she wants to visit!'

'But what am I going to do?'

'Honestly, Morgan, for such a tough business-woman, you're hopelessly unassertive,' said Minty caustically. 'Ring Bethany and tell her that you've been having a look at your diary and actually it's not convenient for her to come and see you.'

'And then she'll suggest another date, and even if I say I'm busy all summer I wouldn't put it past her to "drop in" and snoop anyway. I don't see why I should be driven out of my own home!' grumbled Morgan.

'Well, if you're not prepared to tell her outright that she can't come, you'll just have to put up with it,' said Minty practically. 'It's a pain, but it'll only be for a night. You can just show off the house—she'll be green with envy—and then they'll go and it'll all be over.'

'No, Minty, it will *not* all be over!' Morgan had

been hoping not to tell Minty about the idiot she had made of herself with her stupid pretence about being engaged, but now she had to confess that not only had she repeated the lie, she had claimed to be marrying a man who only that afternoon had told her that he didn't find her attractive. 'And now Bethany wants to meet him when she comes up,' she finished in despair. 'She's going to find out that I'm a sad, pathetic, lonely, desperate liar. Do you think I should just shoot myself now and get it over with?'

'I don't think there's any need for that,' said Minty. 'Look, all you need to do is pretend that Alistair and his children have gone away for the weekend. Say they've had some sort of family crisis.'

'I suppose I could,' said Morgan doubtfully. 'But you know what Bethany's like. She'll poke around and start asking why I don't have any photos of him, and why there isn't any sign of anyone else living with me. I think she'll smell a rat.'

'Hmm, you may be right.' Minty considered for a while. 'In that case, I think your only option is to ask this Alistair to help you out.'

'I can't! He'll think I'm an idiot!'

'It's that or ring Bethany and tell her the truth.'

Morgan rang Alistair.

Her finger shook as she ran it down the names in the telephone directory. This must be it. Brown, A.J., 3 Church St, Ingleton.

Taking a deep breath, she dialled the number. She had to do it now or she would lose her nerve. She must have her story ready and not ramble, or he'd get irritated. She suspected he had a pretty short fuse.

She mustn't sound desperate either. It would be mortifying if he thought she was just looking for an excuse to see him again. He needed to think that she was cool, amused, in control of things. She had to intrigue him without alarming him.

Think of him as a potential investor, Morgan told herself. You've made thousands of deals by impressing people with your coolness and competence. This is just another project you need to make work.

'Alistair Brown.'

Alistair answered the phone brusquely and Morgan immediately turned into a ditzy brunette.

'Oh, hi,' she said, hating how high and silly her voice sounded. 'Er…it's me…Morgan… Morgan Steele. I came to tea this afternoon.'

So much for cool and competent!

'I remember.'

Oh, God, was that amusement or impatience threading his voice? It was impossible to tell. She wished she could see his face.

'The thing is…I wanted to ask you something…well, to suggest something, really, but it's a bit difficult on the phone…. I wondered if by any chance we could meet and talk about it?' she finished, miserably conscious that she had failed in every way to sound as if she were cool, amused or in control of anything except two ridiculously wobbly legs.

There was a pause while Alistair clearly wondered what the hell she was up to.

'All right,' he said cautiously. 'Is it urgent?'

'Well, to me it is,' said Morgan, 'but in the great scheme of things, probably not.'

'What about tomorrow night, then?' he said, and Morgan thought she heard a smile warm his voice. That might have been wishful thinking, though. 'The au pair will be back then, so I could meet you for a drink in the pub. Shall we say nine o'clock?'

Morgan sat at a table in the King's Arms and fiddled nervously with a drinks mat. She felt very conspicuous sitting here on her own. Conversation at the bar had paused when she walked in and although several people had nodded pleasantly she was sure that they were thinking how out of place she looked.

If she wanted to be accepted, she should be at the bar, wearing her oldest jeans and exchanging banter with the landlord as she perched on one of those uncomfortable-looking stools. It must have looked standoffish when she'd headed straight for a table in the corner, Morgan realised, but she didn't want anyone to overhear her conversation with Alistair. It was going to be embarrassing enough as it was.

She glanced at her watch. If he didn't come soon, she was going to lose her nerve. It wasn't as if she didn't have other options. She could sell the Hall, disappear to South America for a year and have plastic surgery so that Bethany would never be able to find her again. That was one.

That was when Alistair walked into the pub. Morgan's heart jerked at the sight of him and the air whooshed out of her lungs. For a sickening moment, she didn't seem to be able to breathe and then everything slammed back into place, leaving her shaken and preternaturally aware of her own body, of the beating of her blood, of the softness of her hair against her cheek and the silkiness of lingerie against her skin, of the odd little trembling deep inside her.

And of Alistair.

Unlike her, he had paused at the bar to exchange greetings with the group gathered there. He was obviously well known, and there was much laughter and shoulder clapping, and then surprise as he noticed Morgan and excused himself.

He walked across the pub to the table in the corner where she sat, chin high and dark eyes apprehensive. For such a tough cookie she seemed strangely vulnerable, and he wondered what she wanted to talk to him about so urgently.

'You haven't got a drink,' he said as he joined her. He sounded irritable.

'I was waiting for you,' said Morgan.

'What do you want? A glass of wine?'

'Yes, but I'll get these…' Morgan made to get up and go to the bar, but Alistair forestalled her by shouting across to the landlord.

'A pint and a glass of white wine over here, Bob!'

The landlord lifted a lazy hand in acknowledgement and Alistair pulled out a stool and sat opposite Morgan, who smiled nervously.

'They seem to know you well here. Do you come here often?'

'I don't leave my children at home while I spend every night in the pub, if that's what you're implying.'

She flushed. 'I didn't mean to imply anything of the kind!'

'I know. Sorry.' Alistair pinched the bridge of his nose. 'I had a conversation with Shelley before I came out,' he explained, 'so I'm not in the best of moods, but it's not fair to take it out on you.'

He blew out a breath and made himself start again. 'To answer your question, I don't come here that often, in fact, but I've lived in this village for twenty years so I know a lot of people, and I've had some good evenings in here.'

The landlord appeared at the table and set down the drinks, taking the opportunity to look curiously at Morgan. 'Shall I put it on your tab?' he asked Alistair, who nodded.

'Thanks, Bob,' he said, and Bob ambled back to the bar while Morgan was still trying to insist on paying. Alistair waved her money aside, though, and she was left feeling foolish.

Why hadn't she bought herself a drink and waited at the bar? Then it would have been easy just to ask him what he wanted when he arrived. As it was, she had put herself under an obligation to him already, which was not a good start. *And* he was in a bad mood.

Morgan wondered if she should just postpone this conversation, but it probably wouldn't improve his temper if she told him that she'd dragged him out for nothing. She would only lose her nerve if she left it any longer, anyway. No, it was now or never.

Alistair took a long drink of beer and set the glass back down on the table. 'So,' he said. 'What's all this about?'

'I was wondering if I could hire you,' she said after a few moments' hesitation.

'*Hire* me?' Alistair frowned, puzzled. 'What as?'

Morgan took a deep breath. 'As my fiancé.'

Alistair stilled in the act of reaching for his glass. 'I don't think I can have heard that right,' he said after a moment.

'I know it sounds mad,' said Morgan quickly, 'but it would just be for a night.'

'A *night*?' Alistair stopped abruptly and his

brows snapped together. He put his glass carefully on the table. 'This isn't something the girls have dreamed up to push us together, is it?' he asked in sudden suspicion.

'No, no… God, no!' she said, appalled. 'No, in fact, the only reason I can ask you at all is because I know you *don't* want to marry me. The last thing I'd want is to hire someone who might think I was just using it as an excuse to get close to him.' She shuddered with embarrassment at the mere thought.

'You and I have already established that we don't find each other attractive,' she reminded him with a level glance, 'and I don't think you're the kind of person who'd make the situation any more awkward than it needed to be.'

'And what makes you think that I'm the kind of person who's up for hire?' he asked in a hard voice.

'Because you said we might be friends,' said Morgan, keeping her gaze steady.

Alistair looked back into the chocolate-brown eyes for a long moment, and then he sighed. 'I think you'd better explain,' he said.

'Well, it's a long story….'

'Somehow I had a feeling it might be,' he said, resigned.

'Basically,' said Morgan, 'I've made the most colossal fool of myself.'

Her honesty appealed to him and he quirked an eyebrow at her. 'This sounds promising!'

Encouraged by the glint of amusement in his eyes, Morgan tried to marshal her thoughts. The only way to convince him to help her was to be completely straight.

'Last October I went to a school reunion,' she began slowly. 'I hated school and didn't want to go but Minty, my twin sister, was dying to catch up on all the gossip.'

'I didn't know that you were a twin,' Alistair interrupted, surprised, and she nodded.

'It's one of the reasons I like Polly and Phoebe,' she said. 'They remind me a bit of Minty and I, although they're much more alike than we were. Nobody ever used to believe that we were twins. We looked so different, for a start. Minty was always the pretty one. She was—is still—very popular and friendly and outgoing, whereas I was always difficult. I was plain and gawky and hated being made to go to parties and play tennis with the other children who didn't like me.'

She grimaced, remembering. 'I would happily have spent my whole childhood and adolescence reading in my room, but Minty and my mother used to drag me out. It was torture. I'd have to go to discos and stand there scowling because I knew nobody would ask me to dance—and of course they never did. It would have taken a brave boy to come up to me with my big nose and beetling brows and bottle-stop glasses!'

Alistair looked at her with interest. She had such a stylish, interesting face now and she seemed so confident that it was hard to imagine her being plain and desperately sensitive about her looks. He wondered if she still felt plain inside.

'Anyway,' said Morgan, feeling as if she was already straying from the point, 'one of our classmates was a girl called Bethany. Bethany was always the prettiest girl in the school. She was tiny with long blond hair which she used to run her fingers through a lot, and she used to make me feel like a galumphing great heffa-lump. She used to pretend to like me, but I'm sure it was only because the contrast we made together reflected so well on her. Next to me, she looked even more exquisite and delicate.'

'Not a friend, then?' said Alistair, following the story of Morgan's teenage trials with more interest than he had expected.

'No, but Bethany didn't bother much with friends, or not female ones, anyway. She was only ever interested in boys, and later men. Talk about being a man's woman! You should see her. When she talks to a man she absolutely *sparkles*.'

Morgan lifted her hands and waggled her fingers in a sparkly way to emphasise the point. 'And of course men lap it up,' she added contemptuously. 'They think she's really sweet and pretty and feminine, but they don't realise that the sparkle switches off the moment she talks to a member of her own sex.'

Uh-oh, she was sounding bitter. Better stop, Morgan told herself.

'Sorry, I know I'm going on about Bethany,' she said after a pause, 'but I wanted you to understand what sort of person she is and how she makes me feel.'

'Shall I take it that she's a cow and makes you feel like you're sixteen all over again?'

Morgan glanced at him, surprised but pleased that he had understood so readily. Paul would have been trying to convince her that she was being irrational.

'Exactly,' she said approvingly. 'Well, anyway,

Bethany was at this reunion. Minty couldn't go because one of her children was ill, but she bullied me into going along anyway.'

Alistair looked amused. 'I hadn't taken you for someone who's easily bullied!'

'Minty's had years of experience,' said Morgan with an ironic look. 'She was desperate to know what had happened to everyone, so I had to go along and give her a full report.'

She hesitated. 'The other thing you need to know is that I was recovering from the break-up of the only long-term relationship I've ever had,' she said evenly.

'The only…?' Alistair looked disbelieving. 'Surely not?'

'Why not?' she countered, chin high. '*You* don't find me attractive, so what makes you think any other man would?'

Alistair felt as if he had been thrown suddenly on the defensive. 'You might not be my type, but that doesn't mean you're not attractive,' he pointed out. 'You are. Very, in fact.'

You're not my type. Yes, she had already got that message, thank you very much, thought Morgan sniffily.

'Well, if any men *did* find me attractive, they were evidently too intimidated to do anything about it,' she said.

CHAPTER FIVE

ALISTAIR studied her thoughtfully. He couldn't be the only man to have noticed those dark eyes and that striking bone structure. And that mouth, wide and generous and unexpectedly sensuous for someone who gave off such a formidable aura.

He didn't think Morgan was intimidating, whatever she said, but he could see that there was something challenging about her. She looked what she was, independent and intelligent, and he guessed she'd be impatient too, of any attempt to play the kind of emotional games Shelley was adept at.

'They wouldn't have thought you were intimidating if they had seen you flat on your face in the middle of an enormous cowpat,' he said.

A reluctant laugh escaped Morgan. 'Perhaps there should have been more cowpats in London. I might have got on better!'

She sighed a little. 'I did wonder sometimes what was so off-putting about me, but there didn't seem much I could do about it. I was pre-occupied with building up the company, and there was so much else going on in my life that finding a man really wasn't a priority.' She shrugged. 'I just assumed it wasn't going to happen for me. And then I met Paul.'

Alistair watched her face as she reached for her wineglass as if for support. She stared down at it, turning the stem between her fingers.

'I'd never been in love before,' she said. 'I fell head over heels for him. I was thirty-seven and in a relationship, and for the first time I realised what all the fuss was about.'

'I gather it didn't last?' said Alistair when she stopped.

Morgan shook her head, her eyes still on the glass. 'No,' she said sadly. 'I was ecstatically happy for a while, and everything seemed to be falling into place. I'd sold the company and I was ready to think about making a life together, but…well, it turned out that Paul wasn't planning a life with me,' she admitted, and Alistair could see what it cost her.

'Anyway,' she went on, managing a twisted

smile, 'maybe you'll understand why I wasn't feeling at my best for the reunion. I'd just been dumped from a very great height by the love of my life, and I was still raw and bruised. My confidence was in the gutter somewhere, so when Bethany zeroed in and went on and on about her husband and family it was like a dentist drilling on a nerve.

'Then she started on me. Was I married? Did I have any children? Oh, I was leaving it quite late, wasn't I?'

Morgan grimaced at the memory. 'She was so *smug*, so patronising about how brave I was to stay single, but all the time *pitying* me... Oh, I can't explain what she was like!' she said in frustration, lifting her eyes to meet Alistair's at last.

'I'd already had two glasses of wine, which didn't help, and I was gulping another back to stop myself poking her in the eye, so I was a bit pissed, which probably accounts for what I did. I suddenly thought, Why should I tell her the truth? Why should I give her the satisfaction of knowing that, no matter how smart my suit and successful my career, deep down I'm still gawky Morgan Steele who never did have a boyfriend?'

Alistair raised an eyebrow. 'So what did you do?'

'I said that as a matter of fact I wasn't going to be single much longer. I told her I'd found the perfect man and that we were madly in love and getting married next year. I suppose I was thinking about Paul, and how much I would have liked it to be true, but there's no real way of excusing it. I lied. It was a really stupid thing to do, and I feel embarrassed even telling you about it—but at least it wiped that pitying smile off her face!' she finished roundly.

'Well, I'm glad about that, at least,' said Alistair, who seemed unfazed by her idiocy. 'Did you then have to make up a whole lot of details about your supposed fiancé too?'

'No, I didn't give her a chance to ask any more,' Morgan confessed. 'I pretended that I'd seen someone I wanted to talk to and I made my escape without telling her anything. I just said something like "wish me joy" and hurried off.'

She bit her lip. 'When I remembered what I'd done the next day, I couldn't understand it. Why do I care what Bethany thinks about me? I should be proud of my life, not ashamed of it, and I was furious with myself for telling such a stupid lie, but I never thought anything would come of it.'

'I presume the reason you're telling me all this now is because something *has* come of it?' said Alistair.

'Yes.' Morgan shifted uncomfortably. She was coming up to the *really* embarrassing bit, and she wasn't looking forward to telling Alistair what she'd done. 'I'd just about stopped cringing and consigned the whole episode to an embarrassing memory when Bethany rang up. She's tracked me down through my sister and wants to come and stay. And, what's more, she wants to meet my fiancé!'

'I don't see the problem,' he said. 'Tell her she can't come.'

'It's easy to *say* that,' said Morgan bitterly, 'but in practice it's a lot harder. Bethany's like a steamroller. She just keeps on going where she wants to go, and won't listen when you try and say no.

'The upshot is that she and her family are coming to stay on May the seventh, and if she sees I'm living on my own it's going to be *so* humiliating. I'd have to either tell her the truth or say that my oh-so-perfect relationship has fallen through, both of which would leave

Bethany in a position to be terribly sympathetic and understanding, and then go home and tell everybody what a sad, pathetic person I am! I just can't stand the thought of it!' Morgan said desperately. 'I thought that if you were there, she need never know that I'd been making it up all along.'

'I can understand why you want to save face,' said Alistair, taking a sip of beer, 'but not why you're asking me to keep your end up. Why not ask someone else?'

'Because you're the only person I know here,' said Morgan. She hesitated. This was the bit she had been dreading. 'And besides, I said it was you.'

Alistair spluttered into his beer. 'You did *what*?' he demanded, coughing.

'You see, Bethany asked your name, and wanted to know all about you,' Morgan tried to explain. 'It's hard to make these things up on the spur of the moment. I suppose your name came into my head because I'd seen you that afternoon and... well, the truth is that I wasn't thinking clearly. I just wanted to get her off the phone, so I said my fiancé's name was Alistair Brown, and that you had two daughters, and that you were all moving into the Hall with me. And now the only thing I can think of to do is to hire you and your family for when she's here.'

There, it was out. She'd said it. Thank God. She might feel a monumental idiot, but at least it was over.

Alistair set his glass carefully on the table. He was looking suddenly grim. 'You're not seriously offering to pay me, are you?'

'Well, it's a lot to ask,' said Morgan. 'You were quite open the other day about not having much spare cash, and I thought you'd be able to get Polly that pony and a computer for Phoebe.'

'A pony—!' He stared at her incredulously. 'How much money are you talking about?'

'As much as you want,' said Morgan frankly. 'Nothing would be too much to spare me Bethany's face when she realises that I've been lying!'

'You really think that I would *sell* my family to you?'

'It would only be for a night, a couple of days at the most,' she said, flinching at the contempt in his voice.

'I don't care if it's for five minutes,' Alistair snarled. 'We're not for sale, and I've got to tell you that I find it pretty offensive that you would think for a moment that we would be. We're not some failing company you can buy up and dispose of when it suits you!'

'I'm sorry,' stammered Morgan in dismay. She had been nervous of asking for his help, but she hadn't thought he'd take it as badly as this. It had been hard to know what he'd been thinking as he'd listened to her pitiful story, but she hadn't sensed that he was *that* unsympathetic. Wrong, clearly. 'I didn't mean to offend you.'

'You know, if you had asked me to help you out as a friend, that would have been OK, but it really gets me when people like you think you can solve every problem by throwing money at it!'

'In my experience that usually works best,' snapped Morgan, losing her temper.

'Well, it hasn't worked this time!'

'No, obviously not!'

They eyed each other with mutual dislike, but it was Morgan who dropped her eyes first. Her shoulders slumped momentarily before she drew a breath and made herself straighten them again.

'Look, I'm sorry,' she said in a different tone. 'You're right, it was crass to offer you money. I had no business giving Bethany your name or talking about you and the girls at all. It was a mistake. In fact, the whole stupid business has been a colossal mistake on my part.'

She mustered a smile. 'I think I'd better go back into business. I never used to make a fool of myself when I just had to deal with money.'

'Then you weren't living properly,' said Alistair unexpectedly. 'The rest of us make stupid mistakes the whole time.'

Morgan didn't believe that he did, but it was nice of him to say so. At least that snarl had gone from his voice and she hoped her apology had defused what might have blown up into a very nasty argument.

She picked up her purse. 'I'm really sorry if I offended you, Alistair. I honestly didn't mean to. And I'm sorry for wasting your time too. I'm sure you've got better things to do than sit here listening to me rambling on.'

Especially when I'm not your type, she added mentally.

'What are you going to do?' Alistair asked as she got to her feet.

'I'm not sure. It may have to be emigration after all,' said Morgan, trying to make light of it. 'I'll think of something, no doubt. Anyway, thanks for listening.'

'Wait.'

He caught her wrist, making up his mind just as she turned to go. 'Don't go just yet. Please,' he added quietly.

Grey eyes looked steadily into brown, until at last Morgan gave a tiny nod.

Only then did Alistair release her arm and she sank slowly back onto the seat. She could feel her wrist burning where his fingers had grasped her. The sensation was tingling all the way up to her shoulder, shivering just below the surface of her skin and making her heart slam against her ribs.

'Look, I'm sorry, too,' he said disarmingly. 'I flew off the handle just now. Money is a fairly sensitive issue for me. It's something Shelley uses to try and gain custody of the girls, and I overreacted.'

Morgan's mouth was dry so she just nodded. In any case, he looked as if he were trying to work something out in his mind, so she didn't think she needed to say anything. She just waited quietly until he was ready to say what he wanted to say.

'How would it be if I posed as your adoring fiancé when this Bethany turns up after all?'

'You mean you'll do it?' asked Morgan excitedly.

'Not for money,' said Alistair. 'Let's leave money out of it. I'll do it if you'll return the favour.'

'Return the favour?' she echoed, puzzled. 'But…you don't want a fiancée.'

'No, but one might come in very handy.' He studied her face, his illuminated by one of his quick, sudden smiles. 'Why don't we have another drink, and I'll tell you what I'm thinking?'

'All right,' said Morgan, adding warningly, 'but I'm getting them this time!'

Alistair rolled his eyes at her determination to keep things fair. 'OK, you go and buy the drinks and I'll try and think this through.'

When Morgan got back to the table with the drinks he looked up with a satisfied expression. 'I think it could work,' he said.

'Good,' she said, setting down the glasses before settling herself back in her seat. 'What could?'

Alistair moved his pint out of the way and leant forward. 'Did I mention that I had a phone call from Shelley before I came out?'

'You did,' said Morgan. 'You said that was why you were in a bad temper.'

'It was. You're not the only one with an unwelcome visitor in May,' he told her. 'Shelley announced tonight that she had booked a flight and was coming over to see the girls. She's in the mood for a showdown,' he said grimly. 'She thinks it's time the girls went to live with her.'

'What do the girls think about that?'

'I haven't told them yet. I don't want to unsettle them unnecessarily. I'd rather find a way to convince Shelley to leave the twins with me.'

Morgan tried to imagine the situation from Shelley's point of view. 'Surely she knows Polly and Phoebe are happy with you?'

'I think she does,' said Alistair, 'but that's exactly what's hard for her. Shelley's never been good at being second best. She wants the girls to love her the most.'

'She should have thought of that before she went off to Spain,' said Morgan tartly, and a faint smile bracketed his mouth.

'Quite. But now she's settled and happy with Jaime, so she can be a proper mother to them again. She argues that she can give them all sorts of advantages that I simply can't afford.'

Morgan's mouth turned down dubiously. 'I don't think that would stand up in court.'

'I'd hope not, but I want to stop her before we get to court. It costs too much money and it always turns nasty, and I don't want to put the girls through that. It would be much better if I can prove to Shelley that I can give them everything that she can. That's where you come in.'

'By being a wealthy fiancée?'

Alistair looked at her approvingly. One thing about Morgan, she was quick.

'Precisely. I think if we were going to get married, the girls and I would move in with you, wouldn't we? There's a lot more room at the Hall.'

'That's true, but wouldn't it be important to keep Phoebe and Polly in the home they've always known to give them a sense of stability?'

Alistair laughed at that. 'I wouldn't fancy my chances of keeping them at home once they got so much as a whiff of a chance to move in with that pool of yours! Shelley knows them well enough not to be in the least surprised that they would be happy to make a move like that.'

'So the idea would be that if you're all living with me, Shelley can't offer them anything they haven't got here with you?'

'That's part of it, certainly, but more importantly you'd be a stable mother figure in their lives. Shelley's big argument is that with the girls coming up to twelve, they're increasingly going to need a woman around. Well, now they'll have you to do all the women's stuff if they need it,' he said with satisfaction.

'Except they won't,' said Morgan and he looked startled.

'What do you mean?'

'It's all very well pretending, but we can't do it for ever. When Shelley goes back to Spain, you'll presumably go home and the girls won't in fact have anyone to do the "women's stuff" with, will they? Maybe they do need a woman closer than their mother. That might be important.'

Alistair looked annoyed at having flaws identified in his plan. 'It's not as important as keeping them with me. The three of us are a team. We've got through the last five years together, and we'll get through the next five, and they can make up their minds then about what they want.

'You've seen them, Morgan,' he said. 'Don't they seem happy and secure to you?'

She nodded. There was no doubt that Polly and Phoebe were happy living with their father.

'Why should they be uprooted from their home and everything that's safe and familiar on the whim of a woman who abandoned them without a thought when it suited her?' Alistair demanded angrily. 'They visit Shelley three times a year— at my expense, I might point out—so they can talk about periods and whatever else women talk about then.'

Morgan held up her hands in a gesture of sub-mission. 'Fair enough. I wasn't trying to belittle your plan. I'm happy to do anything that will help you out, especially since you'll be helping me. I just wondered if you'd thought it through, that's all.'

She hesitated. Alistair was looking forbidding, but he wasn't actually shouting her down, so after a moment she went on.

'It's different with Bethany. She's not impor-tant to me, and after she's gone she need never know the truth. But Shelley is Polly and Phoebe's mother. You won't want to put them in a position where they have to lie to her, so she's going to find out at some point that we're not actually married, and then surely you'll be back where you started?'

'I take your point,' said Alistair, 'but you un-derestimate Shelley's self-absorption. She's not that interested in the girls' lives here. Of course I won't ask the girls to lie to her, but if she sub-

JESSICA HART

131

sequently finds out that we're not in fact living
with you, she'll just put it down to me being
hopeless at relationships. Yes, she might start
pushing for custody again eventually, but the important thing now is to discourage her when she
comes over in May, and I think the best way to
do that is to convince her that you and I are in-
tending to make a life together.'

'How easy is that going to be, though?' asked
Morgan. 'Presumably Shelley knows you quite
well. She must know the kind of women that
appeal to you. Won't she wonder why you're
with someone who's so clearly not your type?'

'If she does, I'll just have to persuade her that
you *are* my type,' said Alistair.

'Do you think you could manage that?' asked
Morgan, not without a certain sarcasm.

'I can if you can manage to persuade her that
someone like you has fallen in love with a
grumpy vet.'

Almost reluctantly, Morgan's eyes met his, and
there was a simmering silence until she made
herself look away.

'I expect that I can if you can,' she said.

Another pause, then Alistair picked up his pint,
determinedly practical.

'OK, so we're agreed. I'll pretend for you if you'll pretend for me. Let's think about the logistics of it all. When did you say your friend was turning up?'

'She's not a *friend*,' said Morgan glumly. 'Her name's Bethany. She's threatening to arrive on May the seventh.'

'Right, so how does that work? Let's imagine we're madly in love and can't bear to spend another five minutes without being together. Do you move in with us, darling, or do we move in with you?'

'Bethany's expecting to stay at Ingleton Hall,' said Morgan in what she hoped was a coolly unconcerned voice, but she was more thrown than she wanted to admit by the casual 'darling' Alistair had tossed in her direction. His tone practically reeked of irony, of course, but still, it sounded odd when he said it to her.

'A big house isn't everything,' said Alistair with mock reproach. 'If you really loved me, you would give up everything, including your smart house, to move in with us, rather than hurt my pride by making me look like a kept man.'

'In the unlikely event that I really loved you, I can't help feeling that I'd still be practical,' said Morgan tartly. 'I've got much more space at the

Hall, and I don't see Bethany being impressed by my sacrifice to move in with you and your au pair.'

'True,' he admitted, 'and the sight of us swanking around your pool is likely to do more to stymie Shelley than finding us all huddled in with Bodil. All right, we'll move in with you and to hell with my pride.'

He glanced at the date on his watch. 'It's not that long until the seventh. We might as well do it next week, so we'll look well established before Bethany turns up. What do you think?'

Next week? It was all very well talking about the pretence in theory, but next week sounded awfully imminent.

But it was her idea, wasn't it?

'OK,' said Morgan, but Alistair picked up on her hesitation.

'You don't sound very sure. Are you losing your nerve already?'

The challenge was enough to bring Morgan's chin up. 'No,' she said quickly. 'It's just…it's hard to keep things like that a secret. Everyone's going to know if you and the girls move in with me.' She threw a surreptitious glance over his shoulder at the bar and leant forward, lowering her voice. 'Aren't they all going to think it's a bit funny? I'm sure they're all looking at you now, wondering what you're doing with me.'

Apparently a stranger to subtlety, Alistair twisted round in his seat and followed Morgan's look, raising a hand in acknowledgement of several nods of recognition.

'What's funny about it?' He turned back to Morgan—having ensured that everyone at the bar knew that they were talking about them, she thought bitterly—and picked up his pint once more. 'We're both free agents. You're a single woman. I'm a single man. As far as people here are concerned, neither of us are involved with anyone else. Why shouldn't we fall in love?'

Morgan turned a beer mat between her fingers, appalled to discover that she couldn't off the top of her head think of a single reason why they shouldn't do just that.

'We don't find each other attractive,' was the best she could come up with.

'Nobody else needs to know that though, do they?' Alistair countered reasonably, unaware, it seemed, of the option to say something along the lines of, I find *you* attractive.

Dream on, thought Morgan with an inner sigh.

'Those people at the bar seemed pretty surprised to see you come over and join me. If
that's the reaction to us having a drink together,
what are they going to think when you move in?'

'I imagine they'll think I'm a fast worker,' said
Alistair. He shrugged. 'What does it matter,
anyway? If anyone asks, which they won't, we'll
just have to give the impression that there's an
irresistible sexual chemistry between us. We
can't keep our hands off each other, so the only
sensible option is to move in together.'

Morgan could feel colour creeping up her neck
at the thought of Alistair not being able to keep
his hands off her, and she willed it to fade before
it reached her cheeks and he wondered why she
was blushing.

'And when Bethany and Shelley have gone,
and you move back into your house, what then?
Do we say all that famous chemistry has fizzled
out?'

'It happens,' said Alistair. He jerked his head
in the direction of the bar. 'I can't see any of that
lot quizzing me about our relationship, can you?
Everyone was very kind when Shelley left, but
nobody asked for the gruesome details. I don't
know how things are in London, but the chances

of anyone asking what happened are remote, I'd say, but if they do we just say it didn't work out.'

'I can't believe they won't wonder,' said Morgan, dissatisfied.

'Maybe they will, but in all honesty most of them will think that you've realised that a country vet like me isn't nearly smart enough for you.'

'Oh, so I get to be the baddy, the nasty city girl who's too grand for plain country folk,' she grumbled. 'Don't you think that's a bit of a cliché?

'Why can't they think that you're too much of a wimp to deal with my success?' she demanded, warming to her theme. 'My money makes you feel resentful and inadequate and, rather than make an effort to be the kind of man who deserves an independent, interesting, challenging woman, you'd settle for an easy life with the au pair who doesn't expect anything other than a monthly wage for running your house and looking after your children. Why won't any of them think *that*?'

'They'll probably see that life with you wouldn't be easy,' said Alistair a little snidely. 'If you carry on like that, I'll get lots of sympathy when our supposed relationship falls through. You've obviously got very exacting standards!'

'There's nothing wrong with having high expectations,' said Morgan, tilting her chin. 'I don't see any point in settling for anything less than the best. I wouldn't when it comes to business or shopping or service of any kind, so why should I accept mediocrity in relationships?'

Alistair looked unconvinced. 'High expectations don't keep you warm at night,' he pointed out. 'You know, there *is* such a thing as compromise. I'm not surprised your relationships fail if you treat them like businesses that fail to deliver on time.'

He was sounding depressingly like her sister. Morgan scowled.

'And you'd know so much about it, having such a stunningly successful relationship history yourself!' she snapped. 'Are low expectations keeping *you* warm at night?'

'How do you know I *haven't* got someone to keep me warm at night?' he countered, and his eyes gleamed as Morgan faltered, obviously trying to remember exactly what he had said.

But she recovered pretty quickly, he had to give her that.

'You wouldn't have asked me to help you convince your ex-wife if you already had a girl-friend,' she said and he pretended to consider that.

'Maybe she's not very suitable,' he suggested. 'Maybe I don't think Shelley will be as impressed by her bed-warming abilities as by your house and your money and the status symbols you've got coming out of your ears.'

Morgan stared at him, not *quite* sure whether he was joking or not. She was pretty certain that he was, but he had one of those faces that gave nothing away and the only way you could tell what he was thinking was to look in his eyes, and she didn't want to do that. Looking into Alistair's eyes tended to have an unnerving effect on her pulse and sent jittery little shivers through her to collect at the base of her spine.

No, eye-contact was definitely off the agenda.

She studied her beer mat instead. '*Do* you think that?' she asked at last.

'Absolutely. Shelley's a sucker for designer labels and all that materialistic stuff. Where do you think the girls get it from?'

'No, I meant, do you have a girlfriend?' said Morgan, pretty certain that Alistair knew perfectly well what she had been asking. But if he wanted her to spell it out, she would.

'Does it matter?'

'I think so,' said Morgan evenly. 'It would

matter to me if I were your girlfriend. I can't imagine being someone who'd be prepared to "keep you warm at night", as you put it, knowing that you weren't prepared to acknowledge me, but if I were, I expect I'd still have feelings and they'd be hurt at the idea that you felt you had to pretend to be engaged to someone else as I wasn't good enough to impress your ex-wife.'

'Well, I can promise you that no one's feelings are being hurt,' Alistair admitted. 'I was only teasing. As you so correctly pointed out, my bed is just as lonely as yours. There's no one.'

'Not even Cathy Reid?'

As soon as the words were out, Morgan regretted them. She hadn't meant to say that at all. Asking about Cathy suggested that she had noticed her with Alistair, and *that* implied that she was somehow interested. Which she wasn't, of course.

Although no one listening to that faint but unmistakable note of jealousy in her voice would have guessed.

Alistair had heard it too, to judge by the strange look he was giving her. 'Why do you say that?' he asked while Morgan cringed inwardly.

She managed a would-be careless shrug. 'You

seemed very close when I saw you the other night at the school.'

He studied her thoughtfully for a long moment while Morgan kept her eyes firmly on her glass and hoped devoutly that her face wasn't as red as it felt.

'We're just friends,' he said eventually. 'I like Cathy a lot but, as you probably gathered the other day, the girls have taken against her.'

Polly and Phoebe, discerning at eleven. Morgan tried not to look too relieved.

'It's a pity in lots of ways,' Alistair went on. '*I* think Cathy would be a perfect stepmother. She's a really nice woman, very attractive, very kind, very down to earth.'

Very unlike *her*, in fact, thought Morgan sourly.

'But for some reason they prefer you,' he finished.

There was no need for him to sound quite so puzzled. Morgan drained the last of her wine.

'There's no accounting for taste.'

Alistair studied her over the rim of his glass. Her chin was tilted at its usual defiant angle and there was a faint flush along her cheekbones. The great dark eyes were bright with challenge, so that she managed to look cross and vibrant and oddly sexy all at the same time.

Something stirred inside Alistair and he felt his pulse quicken. What was that she had said about being an independent, interesting woman? It was true, he thought. Living with Morgan certainly wouldn't be easy, but it would probably never be boring either.

'No,' he said, returning her gaze directly. 'There isn't.'

Oh, God, she had let herself get into one of those eye-contact situations again! Trapped by the keen grey eyes, Morgan longed to be able to look away, but the breath was leaking out of her lungs at a rate that was no less alarming for being quite familiar now. Why did it *do* that? She hated that jittery, jangly, out of control feeling she got when those unnerving eyes were on hers, that sense that the air was too tight to provide enough oxygen.

Of course, breathing would help, Morgan reminded herself belatedly and took a sharp gulp of air. That was better. Really, she was behaving quite out of character at the moment. If she wasn't careful, Alistair would get completely the wrong idea.

She moistened her lips. 'We seem to have

strayed from the subject,' she pointed out, proud of the fact that her voice was hardly shaky at all, which wasn't bad considering that she'd forgotten to breathe until a few seconds ago. 'We're supposed to be talking about this pretence,' she reminded him. 'Are you sure you want to go ahead with it?'

'Are *you*?'

CHAPTER SIX

WAS she? Morgan asked herself honestly. She was someone used to taking calculated risks with money, not with her emotions.

Part of her was backing away, shaking its head and saying, Uh-oh, I think we'd better be ver-ry careful here, while another, rather more alarming, part was prodding her on. Go on, that part was urging. You wanted to change your life. Here's your chance to be different, to take a risk, to be the kind of person you've always wanted to be but never dared to be until now. It'll be fun. It'll be *exciting*. Go for it!

But *would* it be fun? The careful side of Morgan surged back into control. She hardly knew Alistair, after all. It was crazy to invite him into her home and pretend an intimacy that didn't exist. The possibilities for embarrassment and humiliation were endless.

On the other hand, embarrassment and humiliation were a certainty rather than just a possibility if Bethany got so much as a whiff of the true state of affairs.

And she was sick of being cool and careful and in control. Why not take a chance for once and see where it took her? It felt like a big deal, but did it have to be really? Morgan asked herself. Perhaps she was taking it all too seriously? It would only be a question of spending two or three weeks together. As Alistair had pointed out, they were both consenting adults. It wasn't as if their pretence would hurt anyone, and they both had something to gain. What could possibly go wrong?

She took a breath before her careful side could provide a long list of detailed answers to that particular question. 'Yes,' she said, 'I'm sure.'

'Let's do it then,' said Alistair and reached across the table. 'Give me your hand.'

'What for?' she asked, forgetting all her fine resolutions to take a chance without considering all the pros and cons and percentage risks in advance.

He rolled his eyes. 'Don't be so suspicious, woman! Just do it.'

Reluctantly, Morgan put her hand into his and felt his fingers enclose hers with a strong, warm clasp. Before she could protest, he had pulled her hand up to his mouth and pressed his lips to it.

It was the briefest of kisses, but it was enough to send a jolting sensation like an electric shock all the way up Morgan's arm and she only just stopped herself from gasping out loud as she snatched her hand back. As it was, she felt absurdly shaken.

'What was that for?' she demanded, resisting the temptation to cover her skin, which was burning where his mouth had touched it.

Alistair sat back on his stool, looking pleased with himself. 'I thought it would be an appropriate way to seal our bargain,' he said. 'And to start our story rolling. I expect it will be all round the village by morning that the local vet has got his sights set on our newest and richest resident. Then, when we move in together, no one will be at all surprised.'

'I think *I* would be if I'd seen your old-fashioned technique,' said Morgan, who was furious at how casual and relaxed he seemed while her pulse was still zooming and booming at the merest brush of his lips against her hand.

'Maybe things are different in Yorkshire, but in London kissing hands isn't usually considered a sign of irresistible sexual chemistry!'

'Well, I could have grabbed you, bent you over a bar stool and stuck my tongue down your throat in a frenzy of passion,' Alistair acknowledged sarcastically, 'but judging by the way you reacted to a kiss on the hand, I somehow got the impression that you wouldn't have liked that very much! Of course, if I'd known it was what you expected, you being a sophisticated Londoner and all…'

Morgan flushed. The very worst thing was how vividly she could imagine being ravished by him across a bar stool, and now the picture was in her head it was proving impossible to push away.

Almost as bad was being left with nothing to say.

Her eyes slid away from his. She longed to be able to think of something witty and dismissive that would let Alistair know what a ludicrous idea it was that she would even *consider* being kissed by him at all, let alone like that, but her mind was so busy considering exactly that in uncomfortable detail that it was all she could do to say anything at all, let alone something suitably crushing.

'On reflection, I think I prefer the old-fashioned option,' she managed at last, which didn't sound the slightest bit quelling.

'That's what I thought,' said Alistair, finishing his pint and getting to his feet. 'Shall we go? I need to get back to the girls, and I think we've given the pub enough simmering sexual tension for one evening!'

Biting her lip, Morgan gathered up her purse and jacket and stood up as well. She avoided Alistair's eye but she was very conscious of him as they headed towards the door. He wasn't particularly tall, but there was something lean and tough about him and he moved with a kind of easy grace that she envied. Life must be so much easier if you didn't care what you looked like or what anyone else thought of you, as Alistair clearly didn't.

Morgan was still burning from that ridiculously chaste kiss on her hand and she longed to get outside into the darkness, but Alistair, of course, chose to stop and say goodbye to someone at the bar. She was tempted to carry on without him, but that would have looked as if she was cross or upset, so she stood there *feeling* cross and upset and extremely conspicuous instead.

As if belatedly remembering that she was there, Alistair turned and put a hand at the small of her back to draw her into the conversation. He introduced her to a couple of farmers with weather-beaten faces and speculative eyes, and Morgan fixed on a smile, so distracted by the feel of Alistair's hand against her spine that she could hardly string two words together.

It was a relief when he dropped it to demonstrate the size of some pill. Judging by the distance between the finger and thumb that he was holding up, the pill in question was destined for some enormous animal—at least, Morgan hoped it was for an animal; she wouldn't have wanted to be the human who had to take something that size—but she was having trouble following the conversation so couldn't be entirely sure.

The removal of Alistair's hand hadn't made much difference. She could practically feel the imprint of his palm where it had rested against her back, and when he took her elbow to steer her on her heart jumped as if he had taken one of those farmers' electric cattle prods and jabbed her with it.

Oh, God, now they were stopping again. Someone wanted to ask him if he would drop in and look at a pig, and now Alistair was asking about symptoms and nodding with far more sympathy than he had shown poor wheezy Tallulah, and before they knew it everyone else was chiming in with their own stories about sick pigs.

Why didn't they all adjourn to the sty right now? Morgan wondered wildly. They could conduct a joint diagnosis there.

She was desperate to get outside and take this stupid smile off her face. One half of the pub might be talking pigs, but the other half was studying her, and not so surreptitiously either. Morgan could feel her face burning. She had a horrible feeling that there was a flashing neon arrow hovering in the air above her, pointing at her tingling knuckles where Alistair's lips had touched her skin, at her back where his hand had rested against her.

'Do you always run impromptu clinics in the pub?' she demanded irritably when they finally made it outside. 'I thought we were never going to get out of there!'

'Animals aren't sick to order,' Alistair said reasonably. 'I'm not going to tell someone who's worried that they'll have to wait until the morning.'

'Don't you have an emergency service?'

'Of course, and if it was an emergency one of us would go out and treat the animal. But usually, like now, people just want a bit of reassurance. Besides,' he went on, 'I thought it would be a good opportunity to introduce you and give them a hint of what's to come, but I don't know what they're going to think now. You flinched every time I came near you. I think we might have to find another way to convince people that we can't wait to rip each other's clothes off!'

Oops, there went her imagination, working overtime again. Morgan set her teeth and pushed images of the clothes ripping scenario aside with an effort.

'Are you suggesting that I won't be able to play my part convincingly?'

She stalked over to her car, annoyed to find that Alistair was keeping up with her easily. 'You've got to admit that you don't give the impression of someone about to embark on a passionate affair,' he said, not even hurrying. 'You seem very nervous. I don't know how observant Bethany is, but you'll have to do better than that if we want to convince Shelley that we're a genuine couple.'

'I'm not in the least nervous,' said Morgan

coldly as she retrieved her car keys from her jacket pocket. 'I'm quite capable of convincing Shelley, or anyone else come to that.'

Alistair didn't seem convinced. 'Are you sure? Because if it's going to embarrass you whenever I touch you, I think we'd better call a halt to the whole idea right now.'

'Look, I've told you, it's not a problem,' said Morgan crossly. And it was true. She wasn't embarrassed. She was just terrified by the way her body seemed to be reacting to his slightest touch.

Not that she would be admitting *that* to Alistair. A girl had her pride, after all.

'You're not embarrassed?' he persisted, still dubious.

Morgan had had enough. 'Do you want me to prove it?'

Unlocking her car, she tossed her jacket and purse inside and then closed the door once more. 'Here,' she said, and took hold of Alistair's jumper to pull him towards her. Caught unawares, he would have fallen against her if he hadn't put out his hands at the last moment.

As it was, Morgan found herself pinned against the car, his hard body pressing into hers. She could have pushed him away then, but her pride had been hurt and that was always a sore point with her.

She wasn't having Alistair thinking of her as a nervous drip, embarrassed by a tiny kiss. There was no way she was going to think of *herself* like that, Morgan told herself angrily. She was nearly forty, for heaven's sake! She was *not* nervous and she was *not* embarrassed, and if Alistair didn't believe her, she would just have to show him.

So she curled her fingers more tightly into his jumper and pulled him closer still, until the weight of his body pushed her hard against the car and she could feel the handle digging into her somewhere. What with that and Alistair's hand still burning on her skin, her poor old back was taking a bit of a battering tonight.

Then, without giving herself time to hesitate, she leant forward and kissed him full on the mouth. She didn't have to stand on tiptoe or pull his head down. Alistair was the perfect height for her, and when they were standing this close it was no problem at all to kiss him. In fact, it was so easy that it felt astonishingly right, as if they had been put on this earth to do exactly that.

His lips were warm and firm and, after the first

startled moment, she felt him smile, his mouth curving beneath hers, before he kissed her back. She wasn't having that, Morgan decided. *She* was the one doing the kissing here!

So she let go of his jumper and put her arms around his neck instead, melding her body into his and softening her lips to kiss him tantalisingly at first, and then deeper and deeper still, pressing against him hungrily as she explored his mouth and let her hands slide down over his shoulders to encircle his back and pull him even closer.

And the more Morgan kissed him, the more she forgot what she was trying to prove. She forgot how cross Alistair made her, how unsettled and uncomfortable he made her feel, how determined she had been to convince him that she was cool and in control. She forgot everything but this kiss that felt so warm, so sweet, so utterly natural.

Lost in the thudding pleasure of his hard body against hers, Morgan gave herself up to the feel of his lips, to the wicked excitement that flared as Alistair let her go so far and then somehow—she wasn't quite sure how it happened—he was the one in control, and he was kissing her almost ruthlessly, his mouth sure and seductive, his hands insistent as they slid over her, making her shudder with the sheer shocking sensation of being touched by him.

It felt wonderful to kiss and be kissed like this. Morgan lost track of time, as challenge and defiance were swamped by something new and more dangerous...*much* more dangerous. A relentless pounding beat of desire was building between them and it was so tempting to give in to it. It would have been so easy, too, to let herself go and be swept along by the intoxicating rush of hunger, by the searing, spinning swirl of need to hold him tighter, feel him harder, taste him deeper.

But some shred of self-preservation survived and, from somewhere deep inside her, the cool, careful, capable part of Morgan fought back and made her step back from the brink just in time, made her remember who she was and what she was doing and, with a dawning sense of appalled realisation, just who she was doing it with.

Yes, Alistair Brown. The vet who didn't want to marry her and didn't find her attractive. The man there was consequently absolutely no point in falling in love with.

Or kissing.

With a huge effort, Morgan tore her lips from his and slumped back against the car, her body thrumming and her mind whirling. After a tiny moment Alistair stepped away too, widening the gap between them. He looked almost as stunned as Morgan felt.

Drawing a ragged breath, she moistened her lips and forced her voice to steady. 'I think I'll be able to do what's required to convince Shelley,' she said, inwardly marvelling at how cool she sounded under the circumstances. 'Or do you need more proof?'

'No,' said Alistair, and his eyes gleamed suddenly in the dim light of the car park. 'That was quite convincing enough.'

'We're here!'

Polly and Phoebe stood beaming on the doorstep as Morgan opened the door and Tallulah rushed around in circles, barking as if she wasn't sure whether she was supposed to be on guard or allowed to be excited.

'We came on our bikes,' they told her. 'Dad's coming in the car with all our stuff. He'll be here when he's finished packing.'

Ah, she had been wondering where Dad was. Morgan's heart, which had been lurching dementedly around her chest all morning at the prospect of seeing Alistair again, subsided to a slow, sickening thud, although she wasn't sure that wasn't worse. Expecting to see him at the door with the girls, she had steeled herself to be cool and charming, but now that he wasn't here she was going to have to go through the whole process again.

In spite of all her efforts to revert to her usual business-like self, Morgan had grown more and more nervous at the thought of seeing Alistair again. They hadn't met since that kiss in the pub car park, and although she was half afraid of how her treacherous body would react when she did see him, part of her wished she could just get it over with. She would be fine after that.

Or that was what she told herself, anyway.

As it was, they had made all the arrangements for moving in on the phone. Bodil, the au pair, was delighted to be given a holiday and was heading off to Leeds, Alistair had reported, so he would bring the girls and the dogs and enough clothes for a month the following Saturday afternoon. That would mean that they had a week to make the Hall look like a family home and for them all to get used to each other so they could behave more naturally when Bethany arrived. What did Morgan think?

What Morgan really thought was that he had no business sounding so casual and unconcerned when the last time they had spoken they had kissed each other with a hunger that was still beating along her veins. She wanted to ask him if he remembered every moment as vividly as she did, if heat flooded through him at the mere thought of his lips on hers, his hands moving hard over her.

But she didn't, of course. A, it wouldn't have been sensible, and B, deep down she was too afraid that the answer would be no.

'What have you told the girls?' she asked him instead.

'I sat them down and asked them how they'd feel if we all moved in with you for a while,' Alistair said.

'How did they react?'

'They were ecstatic,' he said in a dry voice. 'Even if it hadn't been for the lure of your pool, they were absolutely delighted to be proved right about us.'

'Right?' asked Morgan cautiously.

'I had to pretend their matchmaking had worked, so of course they *loved* that! They made me admit that they had been right all along about us being made for each other, and that you and I were just being stubborn and silly in refusing to admit it. I even had to apologise for doubting them!'

Alistair sounded amused rather than awkward, which meant that Morgan had to be the same. She even managed a laugh, as if equally entertained by the very idea of them actually being in love. Ha, ha.

'You did tell them it was a temporary thing, though?'

'I tried,' said Alistair. 'I explained that we led such different lives, we weren't sure if our relationship would work out, so we were just going to try living together for a month and see how it went. I'm not sure if they believed me, though. They seem convinced that they knew all along that we were made for each other.'

Cue another amused chuckle from Morgan, not quite as convincing as the first, but still, not a bad effort under the circumstances, she thought.

'If we're in love and living together, won't

they expect us to be sleeping together?' she asked, rather proud of her casual manner.

'They're not as sophisticated as they think they are,' said Alistair. 'I can't see them having any problem accepting that we have separate rooms until we're married. To be honest, they're so excited about the idea of moving into the Hall that I don't think they'll give our sleeping arrangements any thought.'

He was certainly right about Polly and Phoebe's excitement.

'We couldn't wait,' Polly explained, 'so Dad said we could come on our own.'

'There wasn't room for the bikes in the car, anyway,' Phoebe added.

Their enthusiasm was hard to resist. Morgan smiled and stepped back to let them into the hall, where they had to stop and make a fuss of Tallulah before they were allowed to go any farther.

They left her panting on the cool tiles, exhausted by all the excitement, as they followed Morgan upstairs. 'I thought you could choose your own bedroom,' she said. 'Do you want one each, or would you rather share?'

Thrilled at being given the choice, the twins

eventually opted to share, and happily helped Morgan to make up their beds.

'Can we choose a room for Dad now?' they asked when they had finished.

'Perhaps he'd like to choose his own,' said Morgan carefully.

'Oh, no, he won't care,' they said with breezy assurance.

Morgan was cajoled into showing them the rest of the bedrooms, including her own.

'Wow, this is so cool!' they gasped, admiring the expanse of lush carpet and the wide, luxurious bed.

Morgan loved her bed, but looking at it now, she was conscious for the first time that it was wasted on one person. It was a bed for making love, for making fantasies come true. A bed for rumpling the sheets and throwing the pillows on the floor and having all that soft space to roll together and slide up and down and—

Her heart was pounding and she caught her breath, making herself stop as she realised just who she was picturing in this imaginary scenario.

'Dad would like this room too,' said Phoebe innocently, and Morgan wondered if they were

quite as unsophisticated about adult relationships as Alistair assumed.

'I'm sure your father would rather have a room
of his own for now,' she said, shocked to find that
her voice was not entirely steady.

At least they seemed to accept that, although
they did choose the room right next door for
Alistair. Morgan would have liked to refuse, but
she couldn't think of a good reason. She could
hardly explain to two little girls how unsettling
she found the thought of him sleeping so close,
how disturbing it would be to lie in her lonely
bed, knowing that he was only a few feet away.

Worse, having helped the girls to make up his
bed, Morgan found herself smoothing down
the bottom sheet and imagining Alistair lying
there, and she snatched her hand away,
blushing ridiculously.

Down below, the distinctive crunch of tyres
on gravel made her heart jerk.

Phoebe rushed to the window. 'It's Dad!' she
cried in delight. 'He's here!'

Both girls galloped down the imposing
wooden staircase, yanked open the genuine
Jacobean door and tumbled outside to jump excitedly around their father as he got out of the

car, talking nineteen to the dozen about how cool Morgan's house was, while Tallulah went into a frenzy of barking and set off the dogs in the car who started baying and yapping in return.

Morgan, having followed more slowly, waited at the top of the steps and watched Alistair walk round to the back of the car, totally unfazed by the noise. It struck her how contained he was, how quietly competent, a still, sharply defined centre to the chaos around him. His presence seemed to throw everything into relief somehow, and Morgan was suddenly acutely aware of the light, of the smell of the grass after that morning's rain, of the gleam of Alistair's smile as he listened to his daughters' chatter.

He opened the back of the car and the two dogs leapt out, rushing off immediately to lift their legs on the nearest available bush, much to Tallulah's indignation. She bustled down the steps to point out just whose garden this was, realising too late just how big the black dog was. Spotting her, Tip bounded over, closely followed by Bert, and Tallulah lost her nerve. She put her tail between her legs and belted back to Morgan, who couldn't help laughing at her hunted expression.

The sound of her laughter made Alistair look

up as he lifted a case from the car, and he saw her standing in front of the door, as dark and stylish as ever. She was wearing one of her elegant little cardigans and a neat skirt that showed off her spectacular legs, but it was her face that startled him. It was alight with amusement and her smile softened the definite lines of her face, making her look younger, warmer, and, yes, much, much *sexier*.

Or was that just because he now knew just how sexy she could be? The breath dried in Alistair's throat as he stared at her, unable to look away. He felt as if he were still reeling from that kiss they had shared in the pub car park. God, how long had it been since he had kissed a girl against a car in the dark? How long since he had felt that heady rush of desire, that startling, almost shocking, excitement?

Too long, obviously.

It had been so unexpected. One minute Morgan had been buttoned up in the pub, so tense that she practically twanged. The next she was pulling him towards her, her lips warm and inviting, letting him discover that she was infinitely softer and sweeter and more seductive than she looked.

Perhaps it was the contrast that had made that kiss so exciting? Alistair had tried over and over again to rationalise his loss of control to himself. She came over as so cool and composed. When he realised that instead of the ice maiden image she liked to project he was holding a fiery, passionate creature in his arms, how was a man supposed to resist? How was he supposed to remember that the kiss was just for show, the way she had clearly been able to without any trouble at all?

He could still hear the coolness of Morgan's voice as she'd pointed out that kissing him had merely been about proving a point. Alistair didn't know why he had been surprised. Morgan had made it plain enough that he wasn't her type. Implicit in their deal was the understanding that there was no risk of complicating the situation by getting emotionally involved.

He certainly didn't want to, Alistair had reminded himself. Even if he had been the kind of guy to push himself where he obviously wasn't wanted, he could see nothing but trouble in falling for a woman like Morgan. They had nothing whatsoever in common. Their lives were absurdly unequal in financial terms, so much so that it was a wonder their paths had crossed at all.

More tellingly, Morgan by her own admission had exacting standards. Alistair had had enough criticism and complaints when he had failed to meet Shelley's expectations, and he was in no hurry to be back in a relationship where he spent his time trying to live up to impossible demands. He had learnt to enjoy an easier life now.

So he'd made a point of behaving as if nothing had happened when he'd rung Morgan. He might be finding it more difficult than expected to get her out of his mind, but no way was he going to embarrass her by letting her guess that. The situation was awkward enough as it was.

No, Alistair decided, it was much better to keep his distance. He was sure that was what Morgan wanted too. They would get through the next month, see off her ghastly school friend and convince Shelley that the girls had plenty of opportunities right where they were. That was all that mattered.

He needed to keep thinking about Polly and Phoebe, who were the only reason he had got involved with Morgan in the first place. Alistair wasn't going to risk making Shelley suspicious by complicating things with Morgan. He would simply stop thinking about her, and once Shelley had gone, he and the twins would move home and carry on as before. It would be fine.

He just hadn't counted on Morgan looking like that when she laughed.

Now she was walking down the steps towards him. Alistair was suddenly conscious of his beaten up estate car and how absurd it looked next to her gleaming Porsche. He wasn't experienced enough on the fashion front to identify the fabrics she was wearing, but he was prepared to bet that silk and cashmere figured largely, unlike his own outfit which consisted of scruffy jeans and a faded cotton T-shirt bought at a rock concert more years ago than he cared to remember. Even his cases looked cheap and battered when Morgan was standing close to them.

'Hello,' she said. There was a decidedly brittle edge to her voice, but Alistair noticed that her chin was tilted at a now familiar angle. She was more nervous than she let on, he thought, and felt a bit better.

'Hi,' he said easily enough after all. 'I see the advance party arrived safely.'

'They did, and they've already been very

helpful in making up the beds,' said Morgan. She peered into his car. 'You don't seem to have much stuff.'

'You'd be surprised,' said Alistair, hauling another case out of the car. 'The girls have got a case each, and I promise you the contents will expand to cover the entire house in no time. It's like magic, isn't it, girls?' he said. 'A few tiny essentials and suddenly—pouf!—they've escaped from the bedroom and are hanging around in the kitchen and the dining room or on the hall floor or hanging off the banisters...'

It was obviously an old complaint, because Polly and Phoebe just rolled their eyes and made nagging motions with their hands. 'Yeah, yeah, yeah,' they said, not listening to a word, and Morgan suppressed a smile.

'Why don't I carry something in?' she offered.

Alistair hadn't been inside the house before. Once, years before, he had come with Shelley to look at the ruined shell of Ingleton Hall, but it had been too dangerous to wander around and he was impressed now to see what Morgan had achieved.

'I feel as if there ought to be a butler, though,' he said, putting down the cases he had carried in and admiring the imposing hall.

HER READY-MADE FAMILY

'That's what *we* said,' Phoebe told him 'We thought Morgan should have servants.'

'She won't need servants while you're here, will she?' said Alistair, tweaking her nose. 'She's got you two to help. That was part of the deal, you know. You and Polly get to do all the house-work!'

Identical faces fell in dismay, then the twins saw that he was joking. 'Oh, *Dad*…!' they cried, leaping on him, and Morgan watched them with a wistful smile. She wished she had had a father like Alistair, who would have teased her and swung her around and gathered her into his arms whenever she needed to know that she was com-pletely safe and loved. Polly and Phoebe had no idea how lucky they were.

They were squealing now, hanging off him, and over their bobbed heads she found herself meeting Alistair's smiling eyes.

Mistake. *Big* mistake.

Off went her heart again, thumping and bumping against her ribs, and her lungs started that silly forgetting to breathe business.

OK, she was not going to spend the next month like this, Morgan told herself sternly. She had to pull herself together. All it took was three simple steps. One, stop looking at Alistair. Two, inflate lungs and breathe normally. Three, carry on as if none of the above has been necessary.

'Girls, why don't you show your dad where your rooms are?' Morgan suggested. 'I'll make some tea.'

Making tea was always a good diversionary action.

The twins were desperate to give their father the full escorted tour and then change into their swimsuits. 'To celebrate,' they begged, so Morgan gave in to their combined entreaties and promised tea by the pool.

'Oh, dear, you look as if you've had an exhaustive tour,' she said to Alistair when he was finally able to collapse into a chair at the poolside.

'We must have looked in every room.' He sighed. 'I hope you weren't expecting to keep anything private?'

'No, I've no hidden secrets,' said Morgan, pouring tea. 'I've always wanted to be mysterious, but sadly, with me what you see is what you get.'

'I wouldn't agree with that at all,' said Alistair without thinking, and she looked up from the teapot, surprised.

'Why not?'

'Well…what you *see* is someone cool and businesslike and more than a little uptight, but actually underneath you're not like that at all.'

Morgan tried an unconvincing laugh as she handed him a cup of tea. 'What on earth makes you say that?'

'Because cool businesslike types don't drink too much and invent imaginary fiancés. They don't give homes to their mothers' fat dogs. They don't fall flat on their faces in cowpats.'

And they don't smile like you, he wanted to add. They don't kiss like you.

'Oh, and they don't grab country vets in pub car parks and kiss them up against their cars,' he said, deciding it would be easier if he could make a joke out of it.

Morgan flushed and bit her lip. 'I'm sorry about that,' she said awkwardly.

'Hey, don't apologise. You were just making a point, and very well you made it too,' said Alistair in a dry voice. 'But don't tell me that you're a simple, straightforward girl, because I won't believe you!'

'Oh, well, maybe I'll get to be mysterious after all,' said Morgan, picking up her own cup and saucer. She wasn't quite ready to meet his eyes, but it felt better now that the subject was out in the open, as it were. Luckily Alistair seemed happy to treat that kiss as a bit of a joke, so she would too.

Joke or not, the silence that followed lengthened alarmingly. 'The girls seem happy,' she said at last, desperate to break it.

'Mmm.' Alistair's gaze rested thoughtfully on his daughters, splashing happily around the pool, but he sounded slightly dubious. 'They seem to be adapting to a life of luxury with terrifying ease. It worries me that they're going to get used to all this,' he confided abruptly.

He waved his arm around the pool area with its gleaming water, luxuriant foliage and stunning tiles. Everything had been done with impeccable taste and with no regard whatsoever to expense.

'It's like stepping into a glossy magazine,' he said, trying to explain his discomfort with it all. 'It's hard to believe Ingleton is just down the road. It feels like a different world here.' He hesitated. 'I guess I'm afraid the girls are going to be dissatisfied when they have to go home to the real world. I don't want them forgetting that ordinary people don't live like this.'

CHAPTER SEVEN

MORGAN put down her tea. 'I'm an ordinary person, Alistair,' she pointed out.

He lifted an eyebrow at her tone. 'No one could ever describe you as ordinary!'

'But I am,' she insisted. 'You only think that because you've only ever seen me in this setting, but I wasn't always rich enough to live like this. I grew up in a much smaller house than yours, and you would have called me very ordinary if you had seen me then. I haven't changed just because I can afford a pool and a Porsche.'

'Haven't you?'

'No. I think I'm the same person I was then. I want the same things as I did. The same things hurt me, the same things give me pleasure—and not all of those can be bought.'

'I suppose you're right,' said Alistair broodingly. 'I've never really worried about it before, but seeing them in a place like this…it makes me realise how many things I just can't give them. I don't mean materialistic things. I mean things like space and opportunities. They can cost as much as ponies and computers, and even those things can't be dismissed as trivial. Who's to say Polly wouldn't grow up to be an Olympic rider or that Phoebe's not destined to be the next Bill Gates?'

'I don't think you should worry,' said Morgan. 'You do what you can, and you can't do more than that. It's hardly a deprived existence, as you said yourself. They live in a perfectly nice house in a beautiful part of the world. Yes, I've got a fabulous house and a fabulous car and I can do whatever I want whenever I want, but the truth is that I envy Polly and Phoebe.'

'*You* do?' Alistair looked astounded. 'What on earth for?'

'Because they've got you.'

Morgan could feel his astonished gaze on her, but she couldn't look at him. She bent to fondle Tallulah's ears. 'I would have given anything to have a father like you,' she said in a low voice. 'I don't remember ever being able to jump on my father. I don't remember laughing with him or hugging him or being teased by him. All I remember is the terrible emptiness in the house when he had gone.'

Alistair studied her averted profile. He could see by the tautness of her throat that it was difficult for her to talk about her father, but he sensed too that it was something that she needed to do.

'What happened to him?' he asked, thinking that her father must have died very suddenly.

'I don't know,' said Morgan. 'He just left one day. He told my mother that he had met someone else and he walked out. We never saw him again.'

'How old were you?' asked Alistair after a shocked moment.

'Ten; just a bit younger than Polly and Phoebe are now.'

Alistair tried, and failed, to imagine walking out on his daughters. 'But...surely he must have tried to see you at least? You don't just abandon your children. Even Shelley didn't do that,' he said with remembered bitterness. 'I'll never be able to understand how she could leave them at all, but at least she didn't cut them out of her life completely.'

'Perhaps it was the only way he could do it,' said

Morgan quietly. 'For years I told myself that my father must have been having a nervous breakdown or something like that, and that as soon as he was better he'd realise what he had done and come back and find us, but he never did.'

Straightening from the dog, Morgan looked blindly out of the window, remembering how desperately she had clung to that dream.

'Now…now I think he was just a man who got bored with his life and decided to try a new one. He was never a particularly hands-on father like you, but he was the only one I had.'

At her feet, Tallulah gave up waiting for another caress and lay down with a sigh, putting her nose on her paws.

Alistair was appalled by what Morgan had told him. No wonder she was prickly and uptight at times.

'How did your mother cope?'

'Badly,' she said succinctly. 'She wasn't well equipped to cope on her own, but not surprisingly she never trusted a man again. She chose to lavish her affection on animals instead— hence the spoiling and the diamond-studded collars,' she added, nodding down at Tallulah.

'And you?' Alistair asked gently.

'Oh, Minty and I were all right. We had each other. Minty dealt with it by simply not thinking about our father or why he had left too much. It's a much better way of coping, I think.'

'How did you cope?'

'I tried to be responsible for everyone. Neither my mother or Minty have ever been practical, so I was the one who sorted out where we could live and made sure Mum paid her bills. She never thought about things like when the bins needed to go out or what we were going to eat that night, so I got used to doing it all instead.

'And that was fine,' she reflected, 'but I think it made me more impatient than I might otherwise have been. It's always seemed to me that if you can see that something needs to be done, you might as well get on and do it—but apparently I'd have got on much better with men if I'd been the helpless type who didn't intimidate them by being perfectly capable of looking after myself!' she added with an ironic glance in Alistair's direction.

'That's where those high standards of yours come from, is it?'

'Probably.' Morgan sobered. 'When I look back now, I think I spent most of my life trying to prove that I didn't need my father just in case he did come back. I guess he's the reason I'm so driven. He sent occasional maintenance cheques for a while, but eventually even those dried up, and we heard that he'd moved to Canada so that seemed to be that.

'Poor Mum did her best, but she was from that generation that had been brought up to think that marriage was a safe career option and she'd never expected to have to go out and earn her living. She had no career, no qualifications, and she found it really hard to even get manual jobs because her voice was too posh and everyone assumed she would look down on them.'

Morgan gave a bitter laugh. 'Chance would have been a fine thing! She really struggled, but she ended up relying more and more on her family, who were incredibly generous and supportive to us all, but still, it was humiliating to always be the poor relations.

'I decided then I was never going to be dependent on anyone else,' she said fiercely. 'And I haven't been. I got a job as soon as I could, and I've worked really hard to make sure I never, ever end up in the situation my mother was in. It meant I was able to make her life comfortable in the end, and to help Minty when *her* husband walked out. We've got security now, and we don't need to rely on any man for it.'

'You've got *financial* security,' he agreed, and Morgan shot him a sharp glance.

'You don't sound as if you think that's enough.'

'I hate to sound touchy feely,' he said with a grimace, 'but when it comes to feeling secure there are more important things than money.'

Morgan sniffed. 'You sound like Minty. You two would get on like a house on fire. She's always going on about emotional security being more important than financial security.'

'She's right,' said Alistair mildly, 'and I speak as someone who knows what it's like to be abandoned too. Oh, not as a child,' he said as Morgan looked at him in startled disbelief. 'But you can feel just as abandoned as an adult when someone you love walks out on you.'

'You mean Shelley?'

He nodded. 'I'm not pretending we didn't have our problems. Shelley was always dissatisfied, always criticising me and what she thought of as my lack of ambition. She couldn't believe that I could be happy to live my life in one place doing a job I enjoyed and thought was important,' he said with a trace of bitterness. 'Shelley always wanted more.'

'More what?'

'More everything,' he said. 'More attention, more money, more excitement, more love, more me… I don't think she'll ever be entirely happy, because she'll always be thinking that there's a little bit extra that she hasn't got for some reason.'

Morgan thought she sounded a pain. 'Why did you love her if she was like that?'

'Because she's very beautiful,' said Alistair simply. 'When we first got together, I couldn't believe that someone like her could really be in love with me. And when she's in a good mood, no one is better fun. She was my wife,' he said as if that explained everything. 'We had a life together and then the girls…it never occurred to me *not* to love her.'

'It must have been a shock when she left, then,' said Morgan, not liking all this talk of how much Alistair had loved Shelley.

'It was. And the girls were so small… I could understand how Shelley could leave me, but not them.'

'How did they react?'

'They seemed to take it in their stride. I think they were small enough to accept what they were told. I told them Mummy was going to live in Spain, and that the three of us would stay at home, and once they'd established that the dogs would be staying too, they seemed to be OK.'

'At least they still see her,' said Morgan, thinking about how much it would have meant to have seen her father, even if it had just been a couple of times a year.

'Yes, they haven't been completely abandoned like you and your sister. They see Shelley regularly and I get them to ring her once a week, so they know she's there if they want her. And I'm prepared to accept that, in her own way, Shelley loves them.'

'But not enough to let her have custody?'

'No.' Alistair's face set in grim lines. 'They're my girls, and I'm not prepared to accept the idea of having a little compartment in my life when I see them and living completely differently the rest of the time. They're part of my whole life, not just a bit of it.

'And they need me,' he went on. 'I'm the one that gives them the emotional security your sister talks about. Shelley can't give them that. I know her, and I know what she's like. She's left them once and she'll leave them again if suits her. She'll always put herself first, and I'll always put the girls first, it's as simple as that.'

Morgan thought of her own father, who had been like Shelley, and felt sad.

'I'm not prepared to risk the girls getting hurt,' Alistair said. 'It would be much harder for them now to be uprooted from everything familiar and have to go and live in a different country with a different language, but that's not the real reason I'll fight Shelley every inch of the way if she persists in trying to get custody. It's because they'll never be able to trust her. She might want them now, but what about when things get difficult? When they become less cute and start turning into stroppy adolescents and bringing home unsuitable boyfriends?

'Shelley's a perfectionist,' he said. 'She'll criticise the girls and they'll have just the kind of arguments she and I used to have, and then she'll lose interest, just the way she lost interest in me. And this time it would hurt them even more.' Alistair's expression hardened. 'I'm not letting her do that to them. Polly and Phoebe are staying with me.'

Morgan watched the two little girls in the pool. They were hanging on to the edge, giggling, utterly oblivious to the two adults and their conversation, and she felt a rush of affection for their breezy insouciance.

'It's very important that we convince Shelley that we've got a genuine relationship, isn't it?' she said to Alistair, and he nodded grimly.

'Yes, it is.'

'I'm glad you told me a bit more about it,' she said. 'The Bethany thing…that's just my pride at stake, but the girls are more important. I just hope we'll be able to carry it off.'

'We're going to have to,' said Alistair. 'It's too late to change our minds, anyway. I've already told Shelley about you.'

'What did you say?' asked Morgan, trying not to appear too interested.

'I said I'd met the most amazing woman and fallen madly in love with her. I said that, even though I'd only known you a short while, I knew that you were the woman I wanted to spend the rest of my life with and that, rather than waste any more time, we were moving in together straight away.'

'Gosh.' Morgan found it hard to imagine

Alistair saying such romantic things without an ironic subtext. 'Did she believe you?'

'No,' he admitted. 'Which means we'll have to work extra hard to convince her that it's true when she's here.'

Morgan suddenly lost her nerve. It was one thing to persuade Bethany that they were in love, quite another to convince Shelley, who must know Alistair very well indeed.

'Do you think we'll be able to do it?' she asked doubtfully.

'We'll have to,' said Alistair. He reached out and took Morgan's hand, curling his fingers warmly around hers. 'Will it really be so hard to pretend that we're in love?' he asked, smiling in a way that made her heart start thumping uncomfortably.

Her mouth felt dry and she moistened her lips surreptitiously. She had a nasty feeling that the hard part might well be remembering that it was all just a pretence.

'I'll do my best,' she said.

Morgan had expected things to change once Alistair and the girls moved in, but she hadn't counted on just what a difference they would make to her life. There were no more solitary suppers with just Talullah, wistfully watching every mouthful, for company, no more quiet evenings reading a book, no more time to sit and wonder what she was doing with her life.

It was like a crash course in motherhood. Morgan had often wondered what it would be like to have a family. Well, now she knew and the answer was exhausting!

Alistair hadn't been joking when he'd said that the contents of the girls' suitcases would expand. Morgan was unprepared for the sheer mess that two smallish girls could generate. Alistair wasn't the tidiest of people either. He was always leaving the newspaper open on the kitchen table and would take something out of the fridge without ever thinking about putting it back when he had finished. Morgan found half finished cups of coffee, scribbled notes and various bits of veterinary equipment all over the house.

Nor did the dogs help. As Alistair had predicted, they had settled down surprisingly quickly with Tallulah, but he hadn't warned her about the hairs Tip shed if you so much as looked at him, or the holes Bert dug in the lawn. Tip liked to bring in sticks which he would chew noisily on the carpets, while Tallulah fell under

Bert's influence and took to scuffing her back legs in the grass, thus adding her share to the muddy footprints that covered the kitchen floor.

For Morgan, used to the calm, orderly existence of living on her own, the constant mess was quite stressful. It would have been easy to spend the entire day cleaning up after them all, but she never seemed to have the time to do more than contain the chaos at a certain level. She was hard put to describe what she did all day now, but there were three dogs to walk and shopping to do and homework to assist and children to be ferried between school and friends and dancing classes.

Alistair had been insistent that she shouldn't do all the washing and cooking as well, but he worked such long hours that it hardly seemed fair to lash him to the stove the moment he walked in the door, by which time the girls were starving. He did cook sometimes, and Morgan enjoyed the plain but nutritious meals he produced, but she soon took over all the washing, having watched him gather up a huge load of coloured and white clothes, shove the whole lot into the machine and then hand the dry items back to the girls without even the suggestion of an iron.

Polly and Phoebe were delighted to have beautifully ironed clothes for a change, but Alistair was appalled.

'I hardly recognized my old checked shirt,' he complained, plucking at its pristine sleeve. 'I hope the girls don't get used to this,' he said. 'There'll be no ironing when we get home.'

He was always saying things like that—*when we get home*—as if he were determined to remind Morgan that their stay was a temporary one. Morgan tried not to think about when they would be gone. Sure, there were occasions when the mess got her down, but there were lots of good things about having a family too. The days might be tiring, but they were never boring.

Morgan liked helping the girls with their homework. She liked the clatter of footsteps on the stairs and the sound of laughter. She liked the feeling that the house was at last becoming a home.

She liked having someone to talk to, someone to argue with, someone to laugh with. The girls were funny and chatty, and Alistair had a caustic wit that Morgan appreciated even if she did often disagree with him. They fell into the habit of sharing a glass of wine after the girls had gone to bed, and usually ended up arguing about something or another, ending up exasperated and stimulated by each other in equal measure.

He was so different from Paul, who was the only other man Morgan had lived with. Paul had always been very fussy about his wine and his food and his clothes. He wore Italian suits and had his shirts hand-made in Jermyn Street, and would spend hours selecting exactly the right wine to go with the meal.

Alistair wandered around barefoot most of the time and, as far as Morgan knew, didn't even possess a tie. He would happily eat baked beans out of the can, or make sandwiches the size of doorsteps to have at the kitchen table with a mug of tea. He was often irritable, if not downright grumpy, but still Morgan was conscious of a curious lightening of the heart when he was in the room, of a shivery sensation in the pit of her stomach and a glow that seeped alarmingly along her veins.

At first Morgan insisted on denying to herself that she was attracted to him at all, and invented all sorts of spurious reasons to explain her un-settling physical reaction to his presence. She was bored, she was ill, she was just on the rebound from Paul. Sometimes she persuaded herself that she was just getting into her role.

But in the end she just had to accept the truth, which was that the more she saw Alistair, the more attractive he seemed. Morgan couldn't believe now that when she had first met him she had dismissed him as being rather ordinary.

Now her eyes would rest on his throat, or the line of his jaw, and she would get a squirmy feeling at the base of her spine. She would look at his hands and imagine how they would feel on her skin and heat would flood through her. She would twitch with the need to reach out and touch him, and all Alistair would have to do was turn his head or smile and the breath would snare in her throat and her mouth would dry.

She was in a bad way, in fact, but Morgan did her best to hide it beneath a brisk manner. It wouldn't have fooled Minty for a minute, but Alistair knew her less well and she was pretty sure he had no idea that she was finding him increasingly irresistible.

She hoped so, anyway.

The nights were nearly as bad as the evenings when he was around. Morgan was agonizingly conscious of him sleeping in the next room. She never went in there, thinking that Alistair deserved his privacy, but she didn't need to. She could already imagine him far too clearly for her own comfort.

Lying in bed, she would think about how close he was and, no matter how much time she spent sternly reminding herself of the reality of the situation, she would always end up fantasising anyway about what it would be like if they were sharing a bed, if he was lying right next to her, close enough for her to lay a hand on his spine, close enough to kiss the back of his neck and slide her arms enticingly around him, close enough for him to roll over and reach for her with a smile... It was Morgan's dark and shameful secret, and every day she vowed to stop her sad little fantasies.

Because the truth was that Alistair never touched her, even by accident. He talked, he smiled, he laughed, but he never touched, and Morgan was too clear-sighted to fool herself that there was any sign that he even wanted to.

It might have helped if she could have felt resentful, but Alistair didn't even give her the satisfaction of being able to complain about him. He was very thoughtful and, perhaps because he had run a household on his own for so long, much more aware than most men Morgan knew of how much extra work the girls and he were creating.

'Why don't I get Bodil back?' he said, frowning as he watched her unload the washing machine one day. 'You're doing too much.'

'It's OK,' said Morgan lightly. 'It's all a novelty for me, remember. And, to be honest,' she added, 'I'm enjoying being busy again. Since the house has been finished and I've moved in, I haven't known what to do with myself. You always think it would be lovely to have nothing to do all day, but it's not so much fun when you're sitting around feeling bored and lonely because everybody else is out at work.'

She began hanging the clothes on the drying rack, ready to hoist it over the state-of-the-art kitchen range. In spite of the fact that it was May, a dreary grey rain was streaking the windows. Phoebe had come home with felt pen marks all over her sweatshirt and Polly had just remembered that it was her dancing class the next day which meant that her leotard needed to be washed *now*.

Morgan had still to get used to their inability to think ahead. Everything was always done at the very last moment, which led to some fairly tense stand-offs with Morgan, who was a planner by nature. A control freak, Minty would say, but Morgan didn't accept that. She just liked to know what was happening in advance so that she could be prepared for it. What was so freakish about that?

'It's different if you've got children,' she went on. 'You're running all day if you've got them to think about, as I'm discovering for myself, but until you and the girls arrived I didn't have anything to do or anyone to look after apart from Tallulah, and it wasn't enough. I like being busy.'

It was Alistair's turn to cook that evening and he was hunting around for a chopping board and a knife. 'Why did you give up your job if you felt like that?'

'It's hard to remember now.' Morgan sighed a little as she shook out the pink leotard to hang in prime position on the rack, while she thought about the buzz of her days at the company, toughing out deals, wheeling and dealing, negotiating, taking risks and feeling the adrenalin surge… It was all a far cry from washing and ironing and walking dogs.

'I think I'd worked so hard and spent so many years building up my company that it felt like part of me,' she said reflectively, 'but I'd got to the point where I'd done the hardest bit. I'd had the idea and developed it and it had been successful beyond my wildest dreams. I'd taken the risks and they'd paid off. I suppose I started to feel…*now what*?'

She draped a succession of little pink knickers—Polly's—on the rack, and bent to fish out Phoebe's. Phoebe preferred purple with little dots on.

'Then I got the offer to buy me out and it was too good to refuse.' Morgan turned a pair of pants the right side out. 'And it seemed a good time to go. I felt as if I had done everything I could there and I needed a new challenge. I was coming up for forty, too, and I suppose I was taking stock, wondering what I was going to do with the rest of my life. And that's when I met Paul…'

Alistair, chopping onions, heard Morgan's voice falter and change slightly at Paul's name, and he glanced at her. Just talking about the man made her face soften, he noted, obscurely dis-

JESSICA HART

gruntled. The generous mouth had a reminiscent curve to it, and the dark eyes a glow that made her look…yes, almost beautiful.

Alistair was conscious of a twinge of envy for the unknown Paul. He must be quite something to make a woman like Morgan look like that, even after hurting her so much.

He remembered what Morgan had told him in the pub, about how much she had loved the other man, and how happy she had been. He would like to see Morgan really happy, Alistair thought. It would be quite something to look at her and know that she was glowing for him. He couldn't imagine walking away from that, as Paul had done.

'It all seemed *meant* somehow,' Morgan was continuing, and out of the corner of his eye Alistair was very aware of her body stooping and stretching gracefully as she bent to the laundry basket and then reached for the rack. 'I was so sure that Paul was the one for me. He was so…perfect.'

Alistair must have given an involuntary snort because she straightened and glanced at him before resuming her task, her face averted. 'Oh, I don't mean that he didn't have faults—he did—but he was perfect for me. He was clever and funny and not in the least bit intimidated by me, the way every other man was.'

She paused with a pair of trousers in her hand, remembering Paul with that familiar twist of her heart. 'I know it's a strange word to use about a man, but he was just so *glamorous*. He was different from the other businessmen I knew. He dressed beautifully, he knew about wine and food and the arts, he wasn't afraid to show his emotions…. Yes, he was perfect.'

Paul sounded a complete poser to Alistair, savagely chopping onions, and very aware suddenly of his bare feet, worn shirt and complete ignorance of the arts. He was planning to open a bottle of red later to have with the spaghetti bolognaise he was making. No doubt Paul would turn up his oh-so-cultivated nose at both.

Unaware of Alistair's down-turned mouth and narrow eyes, Morgan went back to her laundry, her own expression wistful as she remembered how Paul had used to tease her. He had made her feel young and sexy and *alive* in a way that she never had before.

Until Paul, Morgan had never been in love. She had given up expecting it, or even hoping for it, and then suddenly there was Paul and there was nobody else. He had dazzled her, it was the only word for it. Swept off her feet, there had always been an element of unreality to their relationship. Morgan had never quite been able to believe that he was really hers and, in the end, he hadn't been. Her feelings for Alistair were quite different. They had crept up on her when she wasn't noticing and now she was in thrall to a different man in quite a different way.

But one thing was the same. He wasn't hers either.

Spotting a pattern here, Morgan? she asked herself wryly. Do you really want to risk all that pain again? Your heart's still very fragile. Do you really want to give it to a man who has even less interest in you than Paul? Do you want to make a complete and utter fool of yourself *again*?

No, thought not.

Maybe she should think about Paul more often. It was a grand way to put her growing ardour for Alistair into perspective.

'I was so happy with Paul,' Morgan remembered. 'I felt as if I had been waiting my whole life for him to come along, without knowing that's what I was doing. It seemed then that he was the reason I'd never had a proper long-term relationship.' Her mouth twisted. 'I thought it meant that I was destined for him,' she said, mocking herself. 'I thought… I thought that it was my turn at last.'

She laid one of Phoebe's T-shirts carefully on the rack. 'But, as you know, it wasn't my turn at all,' she said.

Alistair looked at her rigid back. He couldn't see her face but he could imagine her expression so clearly, the wide mouth pressed into a determined line, her eyes bleak, her jaw set at that proud angle that never quite disguised how vulnerable she was.

'What happened?' he asked.

'Paul got cold feet,' said Morgan. 'I was full of plans as I sold the company. It was all going to be so perfect. I wouldn't have to think about work or money or security any more. All I had to do was to concentrate on being happy with him. I'd bought this house as a ruin and I thought we could do it up and live in it together, away from the rat race.'

'Sounds a good plan to me,' said Alistair lightly.

Morgan sighed. 'The trouble was that Paul wasn't ready to leave the rat race. He loved

London and he didn't want to change his life or settle down—or, at least, he didn't want to do it with me. In the end,' she said, unable to keep the bitterness from thinning her voice, 'he said that he thought it would be better if I didn't include him in any of my plans.'

Paul had been very nice about it all. There had been no unpleasant scenes, just the dull realisation that he didn't want her enough to stay with her, that he had quite a different life in mind that didn't include her. He had told Morgan that he liked her precisely because she was so cool and self-contained, not needy and emotional like other women he knew, which meant, of course, that she couldn't then scream and shout and cry the way she really wanted to.

'It's not a good feeling, is it?' said Alistair.

'Being rejected?' Morgan sighed. 'No.'

'I know what it's like,' he said. 'And I know what it's like to be dazzled and then to realise that you've fallen for the show and not for what's real.'

Morgan turned with the empty laundry basket under one arm. 'Is that what it was like for you and Shelley?'

He nodded as he scraped the onions from the

board into the frying pan. 'She's very beautiful, you know. I was lost the moment I saw her.'

Morgan hesitated, torn between longing to know more about his ex-wife and not wanting to know how much Alistair had loved her. She had known Shelley was beautiful. Did that mean he was a man who looked for beauty in a woman? In which case, that would certainly rule *her* out. Not that it mattered, of course, as she had already decided that there was no way she was going to risk falling in love again.

Hadn't she?

CHAPTER EIGHT

RIGHT, Morgan reassured herself, but still, it was rude not to show an interest. He had listened to her going on about Paul, after all.

'How did you meet?' she asked, resting the laundry basket on the table and leaning against it. It looked less nosy than pulling up a chair and settling down for a good gossip.

'Ironically—as she always claimed to hate the fact that it was the only entertainment out here—we met in the pub,' said Alistair. 'I hadn't been in Ingleton very long. I was the new boy in the practice and still pretty wet behind the ears,' he remembered ruefully. 'Shelley was staying with a friend whose father owns one of the biggest farms round here. They were just amusing themselves. They were bored with being at home and thought they would dazzle the locals with their sophistication instead.

'They certainly dazzled me,' he admitted. 'I took one look at Shelley and I was a lost man. She had this beautiful blond hair and big blue eyes and a fragile air that made you want to rush out and kill a dragon for her. It conceals a steely determination to always get her own way, but of course I didn't learn that until it was too late.'

The self-mockery in his voice didn't fool Morgan. He had obviously fallen heavily for Shelley, and then his illusions had been shattered. That was always a painful process.

'Why did she marry you if she was just amusing herself?' she asked.

'We had an incredible chemistry between us,' said Alistair slowly. 'I suppose it was that, and also the fact that I offered some kind of security. Shelley doesn't come from nearly as wealthy a background as her friend, and she hadn't got a grand career mapped out. Marriage to me saved her from having to look for a job, if nothing else.'

'But she must have loved you,' Morgan objected. 'Nobody gets married just for security!'

Alistair glanced over his shoulder and lifted an ironical eyebrow. 'Don't they?'

'It's not as if you were some millionaire who

could keep her in the lap of luxury,' she pointed out almost crossly.

'No, I've never been that,' he conceded, turning back to his bolognaise sauce. 'Maybe she did think she loved me, but I think she was confusing love with lust. Of all the things that went wrong in our marriage,' he said dryly, 'sex was never one of them.'

Morgan was glad Alistair was busy stirring mince and not looking at her. She wasn't at all sure how to arrange her face in response to that. It wasn't that she was a prude and objected to his casual reference to sex, but she didn't like the idea of him sharing an incredible sexual chemistry with Shelley.

It just made the complete absence of sexual chemistry he felt for *her* all the more glaring, if not surprising. Because—let's face it, Morgan told herself—if fragile blondes turned him on— and really, how predictable was *that*?—it wasn't likely that plain, stern-looking brunettes would ring any bells with him, was it?

Alistair was still talking about Shelley's decision to marry him. 'I think she was flattered by how bowled over I was, too. It must have seemed then that there was something romantic about marrying a vet and living in the country but, as it turned out, she was bored within a few months.'

'So all that sexual chemistry wasn't enough after all?' said Morgan a little tartly.

'No,' said Alistair. 'I don't think it ever is, do you?'

Morgan thought about her nightly fantasies, about the craving to go over and slide her arms around him and lean against his back. That was just a physical thing, too. Of course it wouldn't be enough.

'No,' she said dully. 'I'm sure you're right.'

'Shelley was always lobbying to move to a city,' Alistair went on. 'To be honest, the twins were a last ditch attempt to save our marriage. Having children together worked for a while but it wasn't enough to keep Shelley in the end. I wouldn't be without Phoebe and Polly for the world now, but those last few years with Shelley were bad. It's hard living with someone when you know in your heart they're just looking for a way to leave you.'

He spoke lightly enough but Morgan could hear the remembered pain in his voice and she thought about what it must have been like for him, knowing that the wife he adored was itching to leave him, feeling the chemistry fizzle out and die, looking at his children and knowing that they weren't going to have the cosy, perfect life the advertisers had sold them.

'I'm sorry,' she said awkwardly.

Of course, what she really wanted to ask was whether he still loved Shelley, but she couldn't think of a way to do that without sounding as if she was asking if he would ever think about loving anyone else. And if he asked who she had in mind, what would she say? Would she suggest herself, for the sake of argument? Morgan could imagine Alistair's appalled expression even now, and she winced at her own foolishness. How many ways did he have to tell her that she just wasn't his type? What would it take to convince her that there was no way someone like her was ever going to figure very highly on Alistair's wish list?

And why should she care whether she did or not?

Bethany rang the next evening. 'Just checking that you're still expecting us on Friday,' she said brightly. 'I can't *wait* to meet Alistair—only man who has ever been good enough for Morgan Steele!'

'I told her you were looking forward to meeting her, too,' Morgan said to Alistair when she reported this conversation, and grinned at his expression of dismay.

'I'd forgotten she was coming so soon,' he admitted.

He had been surprised at how quickly they had all fallen into a routine. Morgan was surprisingly good company. Alistair couldn't say, hand on heart, that she was easy—she had decided opinions about things and wouldn't let him get away with *anything*—but there was a sharpness about her that he found refreshing, if occasionally challenging. She had a self-deprecating wit that disarmed him too, and they were able to make each other laugh even when irritated with each other.

It felt as if they had been together for a lot longer than a week.

'Remind me what story you've told Bethany,' he said to her now. 'Are we supposed to be married?'

'No, we're engaged,' said Morgan. 'We're desperately in love.'

'If we're that in love, why are we messing

around with an engagement? Why haven't I insisted on making you mine already?'

'Because we're planning a perfect wedding in September,' Morgan invented after a moment's thought. 'It's just going to be family and close friends so, whatever you do, don't let her trick you into issuing an invitation,' she warned, 'or we'll really be in trouble. Angling for a wedding invitation is exactly the kind of thing Bethany would do so, if we're not careful, we'll end up having to get married for real, and we don't want that, do we?'

Alistair studied her over the rim of his glass. It never failed to amaze him that Morgan genuinely had no idea what an attractive woman she was. She seemed to think of herself still as a plain teenager, but there was nothing gawky about her now. She was sitting on the other side of the table, dark silky hair tucked behind her ears and the wide mouth tilted humorously. The dark eyes gleamed and her skin glowed. She looked, he thought with a jolt of sudden awareness, relaxed and happy in spite of Bethany's imminent arrival. It was hard to remember now the brittle woman who had stood in his surgery that day. The new Morgan was warmer and softer and easier all round.

And infinitely more disturbing.

'No,' he agreed, his throat suddenly tight. 'We don't want that.'

Afraid all at once to look into her eyes, he let his gaze slide away, drifting down to the elegant hands that were turning her glass absently on the table.

'You're not wearing a ring,' he said almost abruptly.

Morgan looked down at her hands. 'No, I'm not. Why?'

'If this Bethany's as conventional as you say, she's bound to notice that you haven't got an engagement ring.'

It was a good point. A ring, or the lack of it, was *exactly* the kind of thing Bethany would home in on.

'You're right,' said Morgan. 'I'd better buy myself a ring before she gets here.'

A frown touched Alistair's eyes. 'I should buy you the ring,' he said almost curtly.

She looked at him in surprise. 'Under normal circumstances, maybe, but it's not as if it's a real engagement. I'll choose a stonking great diamond so Bethany knows how much you love me!'

'I don't like it,' he said stubbornly.

Morgan eyed him strangely. It wasn't like

Alistair to be sensitive about the disparity in their incomes, but she had the feeling she needed to tread carefully here.

'You can come with me, if you like,' she offered. 'We could choose it together, but I don't think you should waste your money buying an expensive ring that doesn't mean anything.'

'We don't need to buy one,' said Alistair, his expression lightening. 'I've got a better idea.'

'What do you think?' Alistair was surprised at how anxious he felt as he watched Morgan open the battered little box.

He had found her in the kitchen as usual when he came in the next evening. 'I'm sorry I'm a bit late,' he had said. 'I stopped off at home to pick something up.' He had produced the box out of his pocket. 'This is for you,' he said.

Wiping her hands on a tea towel, Morgan took the box with a puzzled look and lifted the lid. The box itself was very old. The brown leather was tarnished and inside the satin cushion, once obviously a bright white, was yellow with age, but in the middle the ring glowed, proudly confident of its own beauty.

'It was my grandmother's,' said Alistair,

wishing that he could read Morgan's face. 'Shelley wanted a new ring, but I've kept it in case either of the girls ever liked it...'

He trailed off, conscious that he was babbling to fill the silence as Morgan looked at the ring. He hadn't realised quite how much he wanted her to like it. It had seemed like a good idea at the time. He had hated the idea of Morgan calmly going off to buy her own ring and when he'd remembered his grandmother's ring he had thought it would be the perfect answer, but now he wondered if she might have preferred to show off some flashy diamonds.

Very slowly, Morgan lifted her eyes from the box to meet his anxious gaze. 'It's beautiful,' she said simply and so sincerely that Alistair felt a rush of disproportionate relief.

'Do you really like it?'

'Of course I do. It's perfect.' Morgan lifted the ring out of the box and held it up to the light. The band was a mellow gold and it was set with a row of sapphires and yellowy diamonds, a little dull with age but all perfectly matched.

'Try it on.'

She slipped the ring on to her third finger. It was the first time she had ever worn an engagement ring and it didn't feel quite the same having to put it on herself, but of *course* Alistair wasn't going to take her hand, look lovingly into her eyes and slide it on to her finger. That was for real engagements, not pretend ones. That was for lovers, not just for show.

Morgan knew it was stupid, but her throat was tight as she looked down at the ring, turning her hand so that the jewels caught the light and trying not to think what it would be like if this was a real engagement, if Alistair *did* love her enough to want to spend the rest of his life with her, as opposed to another two weeks until his ex-wife arrived.

'Does it fit?' Alistair asked, and from somewhere she produced a bright, unconcerned smile.

'Just call me Cinderella!'

Something about her smile made Alistair uneasy. Was she just being polite? 'You don't have to wear it,' he said. 'I just thought…'

Thought *what* exactly? he asked himself. That she would wear the ring because he had given it to her?

'I thought it would be cheaper,' he finished lamely, realising that he couldn't even explain to himself, let alone Morgan, how much he wanted her to wear a ring that he had given her rather than one that she had bought herself.

'Quite,' Morgan agreed, keeping her smile firmly fixed in place. 'There's no point in wasting a thousand pounds on a ring that doesn't mean anything, is there?'

'No,' he said, relieved that she seemed to have accepted his decidedly lame excuse because he certainly didn't have a better one to offer her.

'Anyway, this is much more convincing,' Morgan went on brightly and waggled her ring finger to illustrate the point. 'If Bethany were to get suspicious she'd easily be able to work out that I could afford to buy my own ring, but she would never think you would give me your grandmother's ring unless you really loved me.'

There was a long, long pause. Morgan could hear her words echoing into the suddenly deafening silence and she was gripped by the sudden fear that she had got her intonation wrong and it had all sounded horribly like a question.

You wouldn't have given me this ring unless you loved me, would you? Oh, God, was that what it had sounded like to Alistair? It smacked too much of fishing for compliments and information, and Morgan had always despised people who did that.

If you wanted to know something, she had always believed, you should just ask outright.

So if she wanted to know if Alistair really loved her she would ask him, but there was no point in doing that, because she already knew the answer. He didn't.

Morgan decided to risk a quick glance to see if he was looking as uncomfortable as he would undoubtedly be looking if that was how he *had* heard her, but it was a mistake. Her eyes snagged on his and, once caught, were held, and all thoughts of analysing his expression were swamped in a rush of awareness that left her preternaturally conscious of the beat of her heart and the tingle of her senses, each of which was all at once on full alert.

She could hear the slow tick of the clock in the hall, smell the parmesan she had been grating before Alistair came in, feel the unfamiliar weight of the ring on her finger.

And she could see Alistair outlined in extraordinary detail. It was as if she had only ever seen him blurrily before and now he had snapped into focus so that everything about him was sharply defined: the thickness of his lashes, the lines at the corner of his eyes, the texture of his skin and the way the hair grew at his temples. Until now, she had never noticed the darker ring on the outside of his pupils, throwing the paleness of the grey into startling relief, or that faint scar on his cheek.

'Let's hope it does the trick,' said Alistair.

The sound of his voice, oddly strained, broke the lengthening silence and jolted Morgan out of that unreal feeling, leaving her disorientated for a moment. Trick? What trick? What was he talking about?

Then she remembered Bethany and the ring and she turned back to pick up the grater, ridiculously shaken.

'I'm sure it will,' she said. 'Thank you so much. I'll take great care of it, I promise.'

Alistair looked at Morgan's back. There were things he felt that they should discuss, but there was something discouraging about the set of her shoulders. But if they didn't talk now, the girls would come in and the moment would be lost.

He decided to take the bull by the horns, albeit by a roundabout route.

'Can I do anything to help?' he asked.

'You could peel some potatoes if you like.'

'Fine.' Alistair rolled up his sleeves and

rummaged around in the drawer for the peeler while he tried to think of the best way to approach what was on his mind.

'I've been thinking about Bethany coming tomorrow,' he said at last.

'Oh, yes?'

'I'm wondering if we should sleep together,' he said.

Morgan's hands stilled on the grater.

'I don't mean *sleep* together,' Alistair rushed on, unnerved by the suddenly rigid silence. 'I just mean…you know… share a room.'

'Oh.' Morgan swallowed. She had known that was what he meant, of course, but it took a little time for logic to catch up with the unnervingly vivid picture that had presented itself when he'd suggested sleeping together. 'Do you think that's really necessary?'

'The twins might accept us sharing separate rooms, but someone like Shelley wouldn't find our relationship very convincing unless she did think we were sleeping together,' he said carefully. 'Presumably Bethany would think it a bit odd too, if it's obvious we have separate rooms.'

Morgan had to admit that he had a point. 'She probably would…and Bethany's the kind of person who wouldn't be at all embarrassed about looking in every room and wondering out loud why all your things are in one bedroom and mine in another.'

'So is Shelley. We *could* try pretending that we were saving ourselves for our wedding night but, to be honest, I can't see her buying it.'

No, well, Shelley wouldn't, would she? Morgan thought waspishly, her having had such great sexual chemistry with Alistair and all. If Alistair had suggested going to bed there and then, Morgan would have jumped at it. She had no intention of letting Shelley think that her relationship with Alistair was just a pale imitation of their oh-so-sexually fulfilling marriage.

'It's a good point,' she said, ultra-casual. 'Why don't you move in with me tonight? I've got a very wide bed and there's plenty of room for both of us.'

And there *was*, Morgan reminded herself that night as Alistair brought his things through from his room. It had been no problem to find him a couple of drawers where he could dump a few shirts and, although there was plenty of space in the walk-in wardrobe, he had nothing smart to hang there.

As for the bed, look at it! Ridiculously wide for one person. Alistair could lie on one side and she could lie on the other and they would practically have to shout 'goodnight' across to each other. She would hardly notice he was there.

That didn't stop Morgan feeling absurdly nervous as she shut herself in the *en suite* bathroom that night. She normally slept in the buff, but she certainly wasn't confident enough to get away with that, whatever she might tell herself about the width of the bed.

Instead, she had dug out a nightdress Paul had given her once. It was silk and a lovely midnight-blue colour, but fairly discreet, Morgan decided. At least it wasn't see-through like most of the lingerie Paul had favoured. It had narrow straps and was cut low across the bosom, but was otherwise demure, curving over her hips and falling in a fluid line to her calves.

It had, in fact, seemed a safe choice until she had to put it on and felt it slither down over her body. In the bedroom outside, she could hear Alistair moving around and Morgan's stomach began to churn with nerves.

It was nonsense, of course. She was perfectly capable of walking out in this nightdress. If he chose to look, and there was no reason why he should, Alistair would see less of her than if she was in a swimming costume. All she had to do was to walk over to the bed, pull back the duvet and get in. Not exactly a challenge, was it?

So why did it feel like it was going to be so hard? Morgan looked at the door. If only she didn't feel so naked beneath the nightdress. If only the silk wasn't caressing her skin in quite so suggestive a way. If only she wasn't so suddenly, excruciatingly aware of her own body.

Morgan stood behind the bathroom door and took a deep breath, and then another, and another. She kept reaching for the handle, only to snatch her hand back at the last moment, at which point she had to start the whole deep breathing routine all over again.

She knew that she was being ridiculous. For heaven's sake, they were both nearly forty! There was no need to be carrying on like this. Alistair had made it perfectly clear that she wasn't his type and, even if she were, Morgan didn't think he was the kind of man who would take advantage of a situation. She couldn't imagine him nuzzling up to her and whispering, How about it?

Sadly.

For the truth was that Morgan wasn't worried about Alistair. She was worried about herself. Alistair wasn't the one who had been having secret fantasies about being able to roll over and touch her, about running his hands over her body, about the feel of his lips on her skin.

Morgan gulped. What if she were to roll towards him in her sleep? If she were to wake and find herself pressed against him, would she be able to control her hands and move decorously away with a murmured apology, or would she simply grab him in a frenzy of lust?

Oh, God, *surely* she wouldn't do that, would she?

She would have to make sure that she didn't, Morgan told herself sternly. She would remember Paul and what had happened the last time she had let down her guard and made a fool of herself over a man. That ought to be enough to keep her firmly on her side of the bed. She was absolutely not going through that again.

So there was no problem about jumping into bed with Alistair, was there?

It didn't stop Morgan's hands being slippery on the door knob as she wrenched it open at last and scurried over to the bed and got in, without looking to right or left. Only once she was safely under the duvet did she risk looking for Alistair.

He was standing by the chest of drawers, his arms full of socks and underwear, but if she had been hoping that he would be bowled over by the sight of her nightdress, she was obviously doomed for disappointment. He certainly didn't look like a man who was contemplating tossing his socks aside and hurling himself over to the bed to ravish her. Instead, he was watching her with an expression of impersonal concern, the way he might study a sheep struggling at lambing time, or a horse with colic.

Morgan could see him coming to some kind of decision. Dumping the clothes in a drawer, he came over to sit at the end of the bed and looked at her seriously.

'Are you OK?' he said.

'I'm fine.' Morgan tried for a surprised laugh, but it didn't quite come off and, even if it had, it wouldn't have looked convincing when she was instinctively drawing the duvet up towards her chin. Talk about a dead giveaway.

'There's no need to be nervous,' said Alistair, on whom the duvet pulling had not been lost. 'I promise I won't try and take advantage of you, if that's what you're worried about.' He smiled in an attempt to lighten the atmosphere. 'I'll keep my hands strictly to myself!'

'I'm not worried,' said Morgan sharply, furious with herself for letting Alistair see that she was tense, and with him for commenting on it. 'What on earth have I got to be worried about? Given that we're not the slightest bit attracted to each other, we're hardly likely to have problems keeping our hands off each other, are we?'

'Well, that's what I thought,' he said, missing yet another opportunity to deny that he didn't find her attractive. 'But if it makes you more comfortable, I'm quite happy to sleep on that sofa there,' he said, nodding over towards the fireplace. 'It looks pretty luxurious compared to the beds I'm used to!'

'Don't be ridiculous,' snapped Morgan, feeling foolish and therefore cross. The more Alistair went on about the different sleeping options, the more he was making her feel as if she was making an unnecessary fuss. 'There's no need for that. *I* am perfectly relaxed, I can assure you,' she lied, opting for attack as the best form of defence, 'but if you're worried that I might not be able to keep my hands off you, feel free to put a pillow down the middle of the bed!'

Shaking back her dark hair, she met Alistair's gaze defiantly. Her cheeks were pink, her eyes brilliant, and Alistair thought she looked even more vivid and challenging than normal. In order to prove just how relaxed she was, she had let the duvet slip slightly. He couldn't help noticing her bare shoulders and the curve of her breasts and he was gripped by an acute awareness of the fact that beneath the silky material she was probably naked.

He looked away. 'I'm not afraid of that,' he said, getting to his feet hurriedly and thinking that it might be a different matter for him. Maybe the pillow wasn't such a silly idea after all.

He had found an old pair of pyjamas that he had used to wear when visiting Shelley's parents. The jacket had long disappeared, which was just as well. The bottoms were constricting enough, but they would do to preserve the decencies.

Alistair tried not to think about Morgan in that nightdress as he followed her lead and changed in the bathroom. It would be silk. Morgan was that kind of woman. For someone so uptight she was extraordinarily sensuous, he thought. She always wore soft fabrics that made you think about how it would feel to touch her. He could practically feel the coolness of the silk under his hand as it was, and the way it would slip and slither over her warm skin…

And stop right there, right *now*! Alistair caught himself up sternly. This was *not* the way to be thinking just before he climbed into bed beside Morgan. The last thing he wanted was to embarrass her by letting her know that he was thinking about her in such a deeply inappropriate way.

She had made it plain that she wasn't the slightest bit interested in him, after all. Why *would* she be? Alistair was not an unduly modest man, but it was clear that Morgan was way out of his league. The more he got to know her, the more exceptional he thought she was. She was strong, clever, extraordinarily successful, very attractive, even beautiful at times.

What would a woman like her want with a guy like him, even if she weren't still hankering after the marvellous Paul with his gourmet instincts and wide knowledge of the arts? Of *course* she wouldn't be bothered about sharing a bed with a mere country vet.

Thinking about it, it didn't take Alistair long to conclude that he had misread the situation. It wouldn't be the first time that he had read a woman completely wrong, would it? he thought wryly. Morgan was probably in there fuming at his patronising assumption that she would turn a hair just because he was in the same room.

Alistair grimaced at his reflection in the mirror. Better not apologise, though, he decided. When you were in a hole of your own making, he had learnt that it was best to stop digging.

He would just go out, get into bed beside Morgan and think about Polly and Phoebe, the reason he was there in the first place, and not about how exciting and enticing and inviting she looked in that damned silk nightdress.

'I'll have to leave my phone on, I'm afraid,' he said, setting it down on the bedside table. 'I'm on call tonight.'

'Do you get many emergencies in the middle of the night?' Morgan was relieved to discover that she could make conversation after all. Not very interesting conversation, maybe, but at least she could string some words together and sound relatively normal, which was pretty good given the way all the air in her lungs had evaporated as Alistair had walked out of the bathroom wearing only a pair of very old pyjama bottoms.

She had thought about pretending to be asleep, but then decided that would look silly. On the other hand, she didn't want to look as if she was ogling him, so she had compromised by picking up a book instead and pretending to be absorbed in it.

Pretending being the operative word. The words joggled around on the page and blurred before her eyes while all her attention was riveted on Alistair. One glance had been enough to imprint his image over the print. He was no Mr Universe, that was for sure, but he had a lean, tautly muscled body and broad shoulders that looked more than capable of hauling farm animals around.

And just right for resting one's cheek against.

'Not that often.' Alistair was answering her question as he sat on the edge of the bed with his back to her and set the alarm on his mobile phone. 'But if you do get a call it usually is a real emergency so you have to get up and go, whatever time it is.'

His attention was fixed on his phone, which meant that Morgan could let her eyes rest on his back. It looked warm and firm and solid, and her fingers tingled with the need to reach out and lay her palm against his skin, to feel his muscles flex in response.

What would it be like to be able to do that? What would it be like to know that if she touched him he would smile? To know that if she kneeled behind him and slid her hands under his arms to spread her fingers over his chest she could kiss the nape of his neck, kiss her way up his throat and along his jaw until he turned and kissed her back and pulled her down across the bed…?

Morgan shut her book with a snap.

'Good book?' asked Alistair, who had finished fiddling with the phone and was pulling back the duvet.

'Um…yes,' said Morgan in a high voice, although right at that moment she couldn't remember anything at all about it.

'Don't mind me if you want to read,' he said, reaching out to switch off the lamp beside him. 'The light won't bother me. I can sleep anywhere.'

Morgan put the book down on the bedside table. 'I'm tired anyway,' she said.

'Well…goodnight then.'

'Goodnight.'

She switched off her own light, hoping desperately that it would all seem easier in the dark.

It didn't. She might not be able to see Alistair, or touch him, but she was excruciatingly aware of his warm, solid presence only inches away from her. She could hear him sigh tiredly, feel the mattress shift as he made himself comfortable.

Morgan herself lay rigidly, trying to calm her jangling senses, every nerve straining across the bed to where Alistair might or might not have fallen asleep. His breathing was deep and slow. It *sounded* as if he were sleeping soundly. Morgan didn't know whether to be relieved or annoyed that he had dropped off so easily. Clearly sleeping next to strange women didn't bother *him*.

The tension in her muscles was giving her cramp. Very, very carefully so as not to wake Alistair if he *was* sleeping, she turned over on to her side, but that wasn't comfortable either, so she had to inch her way back again. Then she was hot and had to ease off the duvet.

Oh, God, now she needed to go to the bathroom. For heaven's sake! Morgan fought it for as long as she could, but it was no good. She had to get up and creep her way round the bed to the bathroom, and naturally the flush sounded ten times as loud as normal.

CHAPTER NINE

THOSE first few minutes set the pattern for the hours that followed. Morgan had to get up no less than four times, and when she wasn't over-working the cistern she was in bed, vibrating with the effort of not tossing and turning and burning with a mixture of mortification and exhaustion.

There was no way Alistair could have slept through it all. Once or twice he would sigh and his breathing would change as he turned and settled once more, making Morgan's nerves jump just as she was on the point of dropping off, but otherwise he was doing a remarkably good impression of being sound asleep. Morgan wasn't sure that she wouldn't rather he sat bolt upright and shouted at her for God's sake to be quiet, lie down and *go to sleep*!

Some time in the small hours, though, she

must have drifted off, for she was woken by Alistair asking sleepily what the matter was.

'I don't feel well,' came a small voice from his side of the bed. 'And nor does Polly. She's been sick.'

'All right, sweetheart, I'm coming,' said Alistair, hauling himself upright and keeping his voice low so as not to disturb Morgan. 'Come on, let's get you back to bed.'

Phoebe only made it as far as the door before throwing up violently all over Morgan's bedroom carpet.

'It's OK.' Alistair tried to comfort her as she started to cry, but he wondered whether Morgan had realised quite what she was letting herself in for. The idea of a pretend family was fine when you were sitting round the table having cosy suppers with two cute little girls, but it wasn't so much fun in the middle of the night when they were being sick on your carpets.

Behind him, the bedside light went on and Morgan emerged from under the duvet to take in the scene at a glance.

'Don't worry about it,' she said, her voice still blurry with sleep. 'You look after the girls. I'll clear that up.'

Alistair opened his mouth to tell her to leave it to him, but at that moment he heard Polly calling for him and he had no choice but to pick up Phoebe and hurry down to their bedroom.

'Do you want me to call a doctor?' Morgan appeared in the doorway a few minutes later as Alistair was stripping Polly's bed. The twins were huddled in Phoebe's bed, looking very woebegone.

'I think it's just a bug,' he said. 'We'll see how they are in the morning, but I suspect it's just something that has to work its way through their system. It's a bit messy in the meantime, though, I'm afraid.'

He glanced at Morgan and even frazzled as he was he was able to register how she looked in the blue nightdress, her feet bare and her dark hair tousled.

'I'm sorry I woke you,' he said. 'You go back to bed.'

Morgan didn't even bother to reply to that. 'I'll get you some clean sheets,' she said, adding after a glance at the girls' faces, 'and a couple of buckets.'

Both had been sick again by the time she got back and Alistair was looking decidedly harassed as he tried to clear up the mess and comfort his daughters at the same time.

'Let me do that,' she said, handing him the buckets. 'The girls need you more than the beds do.'

So Alistair sat with an arm around each of his daughters, encouraging them to use the buckets and watching Morgan with a kind of stunned gratitude, tinged with disbelief that he could ever have dismissed her as a spoilt townie. Morgan might have more money than she knew what to do with, she might be fastidious about her house and her dress, but she was also kind and capable and got on and did what needed to be done without fuss.

The worst of the sickness seemed to have passed, and Morgan had just started to put new sheets on Polly's bed when an ominous sound rang down the corridor.

Alistair swore under his breath. 'That's my phone. It would ring now!'

Disentangling himself gently, he went to answer it. When he came back, Morgan had left the bed unfinished and was holding poor Phoebe's head over a bucket. She looked up and met Alistair's eyes as he hesitated in the doorway, reading his expression without difficulty.

'You go,' she said without him needing to say anything. She smiled at the girls. 'Dad's got to go out to an emergency. You'll be OK with me, though, won't you?'

They nodded, still very woebegone.

'I tell you what, why don't you two girls come and get into my bed as a special treat? There's plenty of room for all three of us.'

'And Dad when he gets back?'

Morgan didn't look at Alistair. 'Dad, too,' she said.

It was just after half past four in the morning when Alistair got back and he was bone-tired. He found all three of them in the big bed and he stood for a moment, looking down at them. Phoebe and Polly were sound asleep, sprawled with childish abandon across the bed, and next to them Morgan slept with characteristic neatness and control. In the dim light, Alistair could see the sweep of her dark lashes against her cheek and the pure line of her throat as she sighed and pressed deeper into the pillow.

Alistair was very tired, yet at the same time he felt curiously peaceful. It never occurred to him to go and find another bed. Instead he rolled Polly over towards her sister, stretched out on top of the duvet next to his family, and fell instantly, deeply, asleep.

Morgan had had such great plans to impress Bethany. The house would look wonderful. Alistair would be charming, the twins irresistible. She herself would be exquisitely dressed and she would radiate serenity and graciousness as she effortlessly produced a perfect meal, ran her perfect family and planned her perfect wedding. In short, Bethany would be so bowled over by the perfection of Morgan's life that she would crawl away the next day feeling deeply inadequate about her own.

That was where the plan veered into fantasy, Morgan had to admit. She couldn't imagine Bethany ever feeling inadequate. Somewhat reluctantly, she had downgraded her ambitions to impressing Bethany so much that she would never dare patronise Morgan again.

But, as things turned out, she didn't even manage that.

Woken by Alistair's alarm at quarter past six, Morgan forced herself out of bed and put on the first clothes that came to hand, which happened to be the trousers she had walked the dogs in the day before, liberally splattered with mud, and a white T-shirt from one of her favourite designers, now sadly looking the worse for wear with its garnish of tomato stains and dog hairs.

She fully intended to change before Bethany arrived, of course, but there never seemed to be time. Morgan calculated that she must have had about two and a half hours' sleep, but it felt more like two and a half minutes. She was like a zombie all day, and managed to break two glasses and the toaster before breakfast.

The twins were no longer throwing up every few minutes, which was something, but they were fractious and out of sorts, and that seemed to be the general mood. Even the washing machine got in on the act, throwing a major tantrum in the middle of the wash cycle and spewing soapy water all over the floor.

To make matters worse, it was raining again and the dogs were filthy. Morgan found Tallulah rolling on the bed she had just made up for Bethany and her husband, while Tip chose that day to dig up the bone he had buried in the garden and bring it into the house. She was able to follow his muddy paw-prints from room to room as he searched for a new safe place to store it, eventually settling for the cream sofa in the drawing room.

So much for her perfect house, Morgan thought wearily as she removed the disgusting bone with a grimace and carried it at arm's length back out to the garden.

The perfect meal didn't look as if it was going to materialise either. She dropped a carton of cream on the floor, burnt the pastry and let a pot of potatoes boil dry. Still, there was always a silver cloud, Morgan reminded herself. In this case, it was that she was simply too tired by the time Bethany arrived to care *what* she thought.

'Mwah! Mwah!' Bethany exchanged extravagant air kisses with Morgan before introducing her husband, Hugh, and three immaculate children who looked nervously at Polly and Phoebe as their mother told them all to run along and play.

'Why don't you show them the swimming pool?' Morgan suggested and they trailed off, eyeing each other with mutual wariness. It didn't look like the meeting of kindred spirits, but Morgan wished that she could go with them.

Anything would be better than being stuck with Bethany.

'Where's the gorgeous Alistair?' Bethany asked, brushing fastidiously at her skirt where Tip's enthusiastic welcome had left a generous deposit of dog hairs.

'He's got surgery until six tonight, but he'll be back later.' Morgan resisted the urge to look at her watch and could only be grateful that Alistair wasn't there to hear himself described as gorgeous. She hoped she hadn't described him to Bethany like that. He would have a fit if he knew.

But at least if he was having a fit he would be there to give her some support. Instead she had two hours to get through on her own. What was she going to do with Bethany and Hugh until then?

'Um…what about a cup of tea?' she suggested.

They weren't the kind of people who would happily sweep aside the mess on a kitchen table and settle down with a mug of tea and, besides, the kitchen was an absolute tip, so Morgan showed them into the drawing room. The first thing she saw was Tip's bone, which he had re-covered from where she had thrown it and had deposited, with a certain stubborn aplomb, back in the middle of the hearthrug.

Pushing into the drawing room with the rest of the party, Tip bustled over to it and would probably have offered it to the visitors if Morgan hadn't got there first. She picked it up with one hand, while with the other she quickly turned cushions around to hide muddy paw-prints.

'Sorry,' she muttered as Bethany raised her brows. 'I wasn't expecting you until a bit later.'

'Oh, don't mind us!' said Bethany, flicking some mud off the sofa. 'We're very informal, aren't we, Hugh?'

Hugh, dressed in a suit and tie for a weekend in the country, looked askance at the revolting bone dangling from Morgan's fingers. 'Absolutely,' he said faintly.

Bethany's cool gaze flicked over Morgan's stained and dirty clothes. 'I'm just so pleased you haven't gone to any effort,' she said.

Morgan thought of the beds she had made that morning, of the meal she had prepared, and gritted her teeth. 'I'll go and put the kettle on,' she said, and escaped to the kitchen, accompanied by a slavering Tip, hoping for a chance to get his bone back.

Alistair got back at half past six and, hearing voices in the drawing room, went in to say hello to the much-dreaded visitors. He had opened the door before it occurred to him that Morgan might prefer him to change before the introductions were made, but it was too late by then.

He needn't have worried. His clothes were evidently the last thing on Morgan's mind. Her smile at the sight of him was literally dazzling and the breath caught in Alistair's throat. Didn't she know what it did to him when she smiled like that?

She must, he thought, be very pleased to see him, and he had a moment's regret that he didn't get that smile every time he came home. It was all too obvious that her delight this time was directly related to having been stuck with her unwelcome visitors for the last two hours.

'Here he is!' Morgan had jumped to her feet, and was coming towards him, still smiling, and Alistair didn't even think about what happened next.

Quite instinctively, he reached for her as she neared and drew her towards him so that he could kiss her on the mouth. Afterwards, he thought that a peck on the cheek would probably have been sufficient, but at the time it seemed the most natural thing in the world to pull her into the circle of his arm and capture those warm, inviting lips with his own.

The last time they had kissed, in the pub car park, Alistair had been caught unawares by the excitement that had flared between them, so it wasn't quite such a surprise this time. What did startle him was the piercing sweetness of her kiss, that sense of rightness as she melted into him for a moment, and he felt her, warm and supple and inviting, against him. So he couldn't be expected to let her go immediately, could he? It was only right to deepen the kiss, just a little, to let their lips cling as if they had a will of their own, to savour the taste and the feel of her.

In some dim part of his brain Alistair remembered that they had an audience and it was with more of an effort than he anticipated that he lifted his head at last. He found himself staring down into Morgan's face, where her look of startled recognition mirrored what he was sure his own expression must be.

'Hello,' he said, his voice not nearly as steady as it should have been.

'Hello.' Morgan moistened her lips and made an obvious effort to pull herself together as she turned within the circle of his arm. 'Come and meet Bethany and Hugh,' she said.

Alistair could feel her trembling slightly and he wished he could tell her not to worry, that she could count on him not to let her down. When he thought about how calm and practical Morgan had been the night before when the twins were sick, a little pretence seemed very little to offer in return. Bethany would never guess that they weren't a real couple if he had anything to do with it, he vowed mentally. He was prepared to act his socks off for Morgan, if that was what she needed.

Morgan could tell that Bethany was not impressed by Alistair at first. He clearly didn't fit her notion of what the man of a house like this should look like. Bethany no doubt considered that Hugh looked much more at home here in his striped shirt and public school tie than Alistair in his faded T-shirt and jeans. Morgan looked down at her own grubby outfit and thought with an inward sigh that at least they looked as if they belonged together.

Bethany might have been coolly patronising at first, but Alistair wasn't daunted. He set out to charm her, and Morgan could only marvel as he made her smile, then laugh, until Bethany was positively purring, like a cat basking in the attention. Alistair was flirting with her outright, and right under her husband's nose, too. Morgan was torn between admiration, wonder and a sneaking sense of resentment that he had never made the effort to charm *her* like that.

'You're a lucky girl, Morgan,' said Bethany and Morgan could almost swear that there was a tinge of jealousy in her voice as she tossed back her blond hair and slid Alistair a seductive sideways glance under her infuriatingly long lashes. 'I can quite see why you fell for Alistair so heavily!'

She didn't add, *But I can't understand what he sees in you,* but she might as well have done. Morgan could feel herself bridling, but her retort was forestalled by Alistair, who took her hand in his warm, firm clasp.

'I'm the lucky one,' he said, smiling at Morgan in a way that made her very glad that she was sitting down. It was easier to cope with the sudden dizziness than when she had to rely on her legs to hold her up. Morgan was fairly sure that they wouldn't have done the job right then. Ask them to imitate jelly, or rather insubstantial cotton wool, and her legs could have obliged easily, but walking or standing upright? Absolutely not.

Alistair was still doing his brilliant impersonation of a besotted lover. 'Morgan's a very special lady, as you know, Bethany,' he said.

Bethany's expression suggested that she didn't know anything of the kind. 'Morgan was showing me her engagement ring earlier,' she said. 'I gather it's an antique?'

The lack of enthusiasm in her voice made it clear that she hadn't meant it as a compliment, but Alistair chose to take it as one anyway. 'I'm glad you liked it,' he said cheerfully. 'It belonged to my grandmother. She was an exceptional woman, like Morgan.

'Just going into a shop and buying a ring wouldn't have been special enough,' he confided to Bethany. 'I wanted Morgan to have something unique and original and beautiful.' His voice dropped as he turned to look deep into Morgan's eyes. 'Because that's the way *she* is.'

The expression in the grey gaze as he looked at her shimmered in front of Morgan's eyes for the rest of the evening. Later, she had no clear idea of how she got through it. She supposed she must have cooked, eaten and cleared up, and at some point she did at last manage to go and change out of her dirty clothes, although it was much too late to make an impression on Bethany, who had clearly written her off as a slattern and a lousy housekeeper. She even remembered persuading the children out of the pool, where they seemed to have bonded better than the adults, but the rest of the evening was a blur.

All Morgan could remember of it afterwards was feeling as if she was cut off from everyone else by an invisible barrier, aware only of Alistair, of his smile and his hands and the turn of his head. Every time he spoke his voice reverberated deep inside her. Every time he moved her insides jerked themselves into a knot. Every time she looked at him something clenched at the base of her spine.

Morgan had to concentrate on breathing to replace the air which kept leaking out of her lungs, but it was hard when she was continually distracted by the shivery, jittery sensation just beneath her skin. That *might* have been due to lack of sleep, but deep down Morgan didn't think it was that. She was afraid that it was something else entirely.

That meant that along with remembering to

breathe properly and struggling to stay part of everything that was happening on the other side of that invisible barrier, Morgan had to keep reminding herself that Alistair was only acting. He was doing exactly as she had asked, and convincing Bethany that he loved her. She just had to be careful that she didn't let herself be convinced too.

Most of all, she had to let Alistair know that she was in no danger of mistaking his acting for the real thing.

'You were incredible,' she said when they had finally seen Bethany and Hugh off to bed and had closed the bedroom door with relief.

She was so tired by this stage that it was all she could do to make it over to the bed, kick off her shoes and collapse onto the counterpane. 'I don't think Bethany can understand it, but she certainly doesn't have any idea we're not actually in love.' Morgan managed a bright smile. 'You never told me you were such a good actor!'

'It's not as hard as you think it's going to be once you get into the role,' said Alistair modestly.

Not, *I wasn't acting*, Morgan couldn't help noting.

'Well, I appreciate it,' she said, trying not to

mind. 'Bethany might not be very impressed by me, but she obviously thinks you're great. If she had guessed that we didn't have a real relationship, that would have been the ultimate humiliation and I've been spared that at least, thanks to you.'

'That was the deal, wasn't it?' Alistair sat down on the sofa and began to pull off his socks. 'Besides, it's the least I could do to thank you after last night. There was nothing in our agreement about dealing with my daughters chucking up all over your carpets.'

'I guess clearing up sick comes as part of the package when you take on a family,' said Morgan.

Alistair considered that. 'If you were taking us on for real, maybe,' he said, 'but under the circumstances, I think it was above and beyond the call of duty! We're only here on a temporary package.'

Yes, and she had better not forget that, Morgan told herself as she got ready for bed.

At least tonight she was too tired to feel awkward about sharing the room. Morgan changed in the bathroom as before—she couldn't imagine ever being confident enough to start gaily stripping off her clothes in front of Alistair—but she didn't dither around trying to pluck up the courage to open the door this time. All she wanted to do right then was to get to bed and sleep.

Later, Morgan didn't even remember closing her eyes. She certainly wasn't aware of Alistair getting in beside her, which just went to show how tired she must have been. Instead, exhausted by the last twenty-four hours, she dropped immediately into a deep sleep.

Some time in the small hours, she woke. The summer morning was already dawning but it was still more dark than light, and she lay for a while, drifting between sleep and wakefulness, conscious of warmth and a blissful comfort that she couldn't at first identify.

Gradually, though, Morgan became aware that Alistair's arm was lying heavily over her, holding her into the curve of his body as they lay curled together. She could feel his chest rising and falling steadily against her back, feel the warmth of his bare skin through the silk nightdress, feel his breath on her shoulder…

He was evidently sound asleep. It probably wouldn't have been hard to get him to roll over in his sleep, or she could have woken him up. She could move away herself, Morgan realised.

But she didn't want to.

She wanted to stay right where she was, feeling warm and safe in the shelter of his body. She didn't want to lie alone on the edge of the bed. She wanted to be able to snuggle closer, to turn into him and hold him close. She wanted to be able to wake him with kisses and make love in the dawn light.

She wanted to spend the rest of her life like this, with Alistair, and the girls sleeping down the corridor. She didn't want a temporary package. She wanted it to be for ever.

She was in love with him. In the early morning light, it was so obvious to Morgan that she didn't even try to fight the realisation. She was surprised only that it had taken her so long to recognize it. She had been falling in love with Alistair since she met him.

Vaguely, Morgan wondered if there had been a time when she could have stopped herself, but if there had she had missed it. It was too late now.

This wasn't the heady, exhilarating rush she had felt when she'd fallen in love with Paul. That had been romantic and exciting and dazzling, as if she had found herself suddenly living in a dream. Half the time, being with Paul hadn't felt quite real.

Loving Alistair was different. It was more like an insistent beat deep inside her, the knowledge, the utter certainty, that this was it and there was nothing she could do about it.

Morgan listened to him breathing and felt him warm and solid against her, and her heart swelled. *Alistair*. So it was him.

She wished that she could shake him awake and tell him how she felt. She wanted to tell him how her whole world had suddenly changed, how it seemed as if everything had been thrown into the air and had fallen back into place around him. She could whisper in his ear and tell him that she was half giddy with joy, half fearful at the sheer power of the feelings consuming her.

But she couldn't tell him that, could she? Not even in a whisper. Cold reality began to seep back as Morgan lay and stared at the steadily lightening chink between the curtains. Alistair had made it perfectly clear that as far as he was concerned, any relationship they might have was purely make-believe, and temporary at that. If she blurted out now that she was in love with him, he would recoil in horror. Love had most definitely not been part of the deal.

On the *other* hand... It was impossible to

ignore the hopeful little voice inside her that pointed out that neither of them was actually committed to anyone else. And there had been a definite spark each time they had kissed. Why shouldn't they think about making pretence into reality somewhere along the line?

So she wasn't his type? She would never have thought that he was *her* type and she had changed her mind, hadn't she? Maybe Alistair would change his…

Morgan let her fingers caress Alistair's arm lightly as she lay plotting her strategy. Minty would no doubt tell her that she was treating her love for him like a new business project, but Morgan didn't know any other way to be. She hated the uncertainty of not knowing where she was going or what she was trying to do.

There was no point in saying anything just yet, she decided. That would just make things awkward, and put Alistair on the spot. The important thing was for them to stay together as long as possible. Surely if they kept sharing a bed like this, *something* would happen? Even Alistair would find it hard to resist the intimacy of sleeping together every night. There would be plenty of opportunities for her to get closer,

Morgan reasoned. With any luck, she wouldn't even need to say anything. They could make love and let their bodies do the talking.

A slow shiver of anticipation snaked its way down Morgan's spine at the very thought.

'What time is Bethany leaving?' asked Alistair the next morning as he came out of the bathroom, still shaving.

Morgan was drying her hair in front of the mirror. She could see him moving around the room behind her, running the razor over his jaw, buttoning up his shirt, searching for his socks. The situation was so intimate that she felt suddenly paralysed by shyness. It was one thing to map out careful strategies, quite another to keep her feelings under control in the clear light of day.

Terrified that her new feelings would show on her face somehow, and scare him off before she had a chance to put her plan into action, Morgan concentrated on her hair and tried to keep her voice cool.

'After breakfast, I hope. Bethany said yesterday that they want to stop off for lunch in Derbyshire on their way south.'

'In that case, I'll come up after they've gone and move my stuff out then.'

Very carefully, Morgan unpinned some hair and curled it around the brush. She might not get a better opening than this. 'Why don't you leave it here?' she said as casually as she could.

'I haven't got much.' Alistair was pulling on some socks. 'It won't take long to shift it back next door.'

She took a breath. 'No, I meant, why don't you stay until Shelley arrives?'

'But that's not for another couple of weeks,' he objected.

'I know…but it's difficult to get used to sharing a bed, isn't it? I just wondered if it would be easier if we stayed as we are.' Morgan avoided Alistair's eye in the mirror and moved on to another section of hair. 'It would seem quite natural to be sleeping together by the time Shelley arrived. That might be more convincing.'

Alistair looked at Morgan's straight back. She was wearing stone-coloured trousers and a crisp white shirt, and her hair where she had dried it swung in a dark shining bob. She sounded as cool and practical as she looked.

He would really like to be cool and practical

himself, but it was hard when all he could think about was how she looked in that nightdress and, even more disturbing, how she had felt. Once or twice in the night he had surfaced to find Morgan lying softly against him and he had been excruciatingly aware of her warmth, of the silky tickle of her hair and the faint, elusive, expensive fragrance she always wore.

He had had to lie there, gritting his jaw and trying not to think about how it would feel to be able to roll her beneath him, to ruck up the silk nightdress and feel it slithering over her soft skin, to explore her and unlock her…

Alistair swallowed hard just thinking about it now in the cold light of day. There was no way he would be able to control himself night after night. It would be torture to lie next to her and not be able to touch her.

'I don't think that's a good idea,' he said more abruptly than he had intended. 'Shelley won't be here for a while and there's no point in sharing a room for the sake of it. We'd be better off with our own space.'

Well, what could she say to *that*? Dull colour crept up Morgan's throat. Alistair had sounded so categorical that she had a horrible feeling that he might have guessed just how much she had wanted him to agree.

'It was just a thought,' she said.

'We don't even know if Shelley will stay here at all,' he pointed out. 'I did invite her as you suggested, but she might choose to stay in a hotel, in which case it would just be a waste of time for us to go through all the bother of sharing a bed now. I can just move my stuff in here if it seems like she might be snooping.'

'Fine,' said Morgan.

Alistair regarded her back warily. Something about the set of her shoulders told him that he had made a mistake somewhere along the line, but he didn't see how. He would have thought Morgan would be delighted to have her bed back to herself.

'Is that OK with you?' he asked cautiously.

What did he want her to say? *No, it's not OK. It's a horrible idea that means I'll never be able to sleep with you again?*

'Of course.' Morgan clicked off the hairdryer and turned with a brilliant smile. 'Sounds good to me. Now, I'd better go and do something about breakfast.'

So much for her strategy, she thought miserably as they stood on the steps and waved Bethany and her family off. She should have known that it wouldn't work. It was time to accept that she was a complete and utter failure on the relationship front and stop dreaming that things might, just once, work out for her.

When would she get it into her thick head that Alistair wasn't interested? Morgan wondered bitterly. If he had felt the smallest flicker, surely he would have jumped at the chance of sleeping together? As it was, he might as well have told her to keep her fantasies to herself.

The more Morgan thought about it, the more humiliated she felt. She replayed the conversation over and over again in her head, in the end convincing herself that she had practically laid herself out on a plate for Alistair, only to be flatly rejected.

Determined not to expose herself to that kind of rejection again, Morgan took her hopeless love and her wounded pride and retreated behind a barrier of rather prickly politeness.

It was hard to know whether Alistair noticed, even harder to guess whether he cared. He was as polite as her, but Morgan couldn't read his expression. The only time they were able to talk naturally was when Polly and Phoebe were there. Then it was OK, they could even laugh together, but the moment they were on their own, the conversation which had been so easy before would evaporate, the air would tighten until it jangled with tension, and one of them would have to make an excuse and leave.

CHAPTER TEN

MORGAN was dreading Shelley's visit, but there was a part of her that longed for it too. At least it would mean that this awful, tense limbo period would be over. She didn't think she could go on living with Alistair like this, loving him but unable to touch him, unable to tell him how she felt, unable to love him the way she so desperately wanted to.

She had to talk to him once Shelley had gone, Morgan decided. Perhaps then she could tell him how she felt and ask him if he would consider staying. He might say no—he probably would—but at least she would know, one way or the other.

In the end, Shelley opted to stay at Ingleton Hall for a night before she took Phoebe and Polly away for the half-term week. Unlike Bethany's visit, everything went perfectly. There were no crises the night before. The dogs were perfectly behaved, the house immaculate and dinner delicious. The girls were at their enchanting best and Morgan had plenty of time to get ready before Shelley's arrival.

That didn't stop her feeling gauche and unattractive the moment she stood next to Shelley, of course. Alistair had told her that his ex-wife was beautiful, but Morgan was still unprepared for Shelley's exquisite skin, model figure and careless glamour.

She was no dumb blonde, though. Several times, Morgan caught her watching the two of them with a speculative expression. Morgan wasn't surprised that the other woman should be unconvinced. It had been much easier to pretend that they were in love when Bethany had been there, for some reason. This time they were both awkward and it felt as if it must be obvious that they were playing a part.

Remembering the performance Alistair had put on for her, Morgan made the effort to do the same for him. She tried to touch him casually, to rest her hand on his shoulder when she passed, for instance, or to lean affectionately against him, but he was tense and unresponsive and she was sure that he had to stop himself from flinching away once or twice.

Morgan's confidence, always fragile when it came to men, faltered and promptly took a nose-dive. Why was Alistair so remote when it was so important to him to convince his ex-wife that Morgan was the new woman in his life? Could it be that he was still in love with Shelley after all? Did it hurt him just to see her there, a bitter reminder of all that he had lost?

The contrast between the two women could hardly have been clearer, Morgan thought dully. The one so beautiful and feminine, the other so…not. Shelley made her feel more prickly and angular and difficult than ever. Alistair could hardly fail to notice it too.

Oddly, Shelley didn't seem to notice the blatant differences between them. Instead, she appeared to have decided that she and Morgan were kindred spirits.

'We've both made a success of our lives,' she declared as she sat at the kitchen table, allegedly helping Morgan with the dinner. 'We've got things to be proud of. I've built up a business in Spain with Jaime. We're about to open another hotel. It's going to be the biggest and the best on the Costa Brava,' she said.

'Congratulations,' murmured Morgan, wondering privately how you could be more proud of a hotel than your own daughters. Didn't Polly and Phoebe rate in their mother's scale of achievements? 'You must be proud of the girls too,' she reminded Shelley.

Shelley shook back her hair complacently. 'Oh, I am…but I'm afraid they're going to take after their father. They don't seem to have any *drive*.'

Morgan thought of the way the twins had gone about meeting her and setting her up on a blind date with Alistair. It seemed to her that they were both more than capable of getting what they wanted out of life.

'That's the trouble with Alistair,' Shelley was complaining. 'He's got the ambition of a slug. You'll find that out for yourself. It used to drive me mad,' she confided. 'Alistair just doesn't understand about wanting to make something of yourself. He's got no idea about developing his career, for instance.'

'He doesn't need to,' said Morgan defensively. 'He's already doing exactly what he wants to do.'

'Yes, he's perfectly happy pottering around sheep and cows all day.' Shelley's expression was dismissive. 'He's been here for *years*. He could get on, move to a bigger and better practice, for instance, but no! He just stays here, seeing the same old animals, visiting the same farms, meeting the same people. It's all so *boring*!'

She sighed. 'That's why I wanted the girls to live with me. They're growing up in a rut.'

'They're very happy with Alistair,' said Morgan carefully.

'They're happy now they're with *you*,' Shelley corrected her with a sharp look. 'They can't stop talking about living here. Of course they love the pool and the grounds! Alistair can't give them anything like that on his own, but now that he's marrying you… Well, I can see that's it's all very different now.'

In other words, Alistair was only interested in her money. Was that how she was supposed to take that? Morgan chopped parsley crossly. It would have been hurtful if she hadn't known the truth, which was that he wasn't interested in her at all, not even for her money.

The house felt unbearably empty when Shelley

took the girls away. It was a very strange week. Alistair had to wait until they came back before he could move out, but he spent as little time at the Hall as possible. He worked late or made excuses to be out. Morgan took herself to the theatre in York and felt so lonely and miserable without the three of them that her throat ached with the effort of not crying.

It was only going to get worse too. The days were ticking away. Soon Shelley would be gone, and Alistair would take Polly and Phoebe and the dogs and go home. Morgan didn't know how she was going to be able to bear it.

Her eyes stung with tears as she welcomed the girls home at the end of that long, long week. 'I've missed you,' she told them.

'We've missed you, too,' they assured her, then rather spoiled the effect by instantly asking if they could have a swim before supper. Morgan was left wondering sadly whether they had missed the pool more than her.

She was dully dead-heading roses on the terrace and listening to the squeals and splashes from the pool when Alistair sought her out for the first time in a week.

'Shelley's agreed not to apply for new custody

arrangements,' he said, although he didn't sound as jubilant as he should have done.

'That's good news,' said Morgan, letting the petals drift through her fingers to the paving stones. 'What made her change her mind?'

'You.'

Startled, she glanced up. *'Me?'*

'It was partly the girls,' Alistair conceded. 'I think Shelley found them more of a handful this time, and it no doubt occurred to her that they might disrupt her perfect life in Spain with Jaime if she had them to live with her permanently, but you were the one who made the difference.'

'We convinced her that we were getting married?' Morgan couldn't quite keep the surprise out of her voice. She hadn't thought their performance had been good enough to fool Shelley completely.

'It seems so.' Alistair's voice was remote. 'It wasn't just the fact that there would be a woman in their lives from now on, though. What really swung it for Shelley was the kind of woman you are. She'd read about you in magazines and is very impressed by you. She told me that she was glad Polly and Phoebe would grow up with you providing a good role model as a successful career woman who can give them a glimpse of life beyond Askerby. She liked you a lot.'

Somehow it didn't sound like a compliment. Morgan wanted to shout that she wasn't like Shelley, whatever he thought. She didn't think success was about money or the kudos of opening a new hotel. It was about love and happiness and security. She could offer the girls a much better role model as a wife and a stepmother than as a career woman.

But she didn't think Alistair would want to hear that.

Morgan went back to dead-heading. 'What's going to happen when Shelley finds out that we're not getting married after all?'

'I'll have to worry about that when it happens.' Alistair brushed that aside with an irritable gesture. 'My guess is that it doesn't really suit her to pursue custody for the moment. Together we've convinced her that I'm serious about making a life with another woman. If it's not you in the end, it'll be someone else.'

Yes, she could see that happening, thought Morgan bleakly. Alistair would find someone else, someone softer and warmer and more feminine, and she would be left to get by on her own. It seemed to be her fate to always give way to someone else.

'Anyway, it's not your problem,' Alistair continued briskly. 'You've done what you promised, and brilliantly. Thank you very much for that, but now it's time we were out of your hair.'

Morgan's grasp on the secateurs faltered. 'You're going then?'

'I think I'll take the girls back tomorrow. They need to get used to life without a pool.'

And she would have to get used to life without them.

So this was it. A lead weight was settling on Morgan's heart, so black and cold and heavy that she was afraid she would simply buckle beneath it, but she made herself straighten and even managed a sort of smile.

'In that case, we'd better have that bust-up now,' she said brightly. 'We'll need to be able to explain why you've moved out again. It'll be obvious that our relationship has been a disaster. Perhaps you could tell people that I'm too demanding?'

Alistair looked at her and thought that he had rarely met a woman who was *less* demanding. She was so competent, so used to looking after herself, that she had asked for nothing and done everything. Without making a fuss about it, she had cooked and cleaned and ferried the girls around and listened to them and walked the dogs…and somehow, without him noticing, she had come to be an integral part of all their lives.

And then she had withdrawn. Oh, she was still great with the girls, but with him she had retreated behind a barrier of cool politeness which had effectively put him at a distance. To be honest, Alistair had welcomed it at first. He had come dangerously close to losing control of his feelings for her. He couldn't get the feel of her out of his mind. He kept thinking about how good it had felt to kiss her. He would look at her and think about undressing her, about pulling her towards him, making her smile, tangling his fingers in the silky hair…

But she was difficult, Alistair would remind himself whenever the fantasies threatened to overwhelm him. She was prickly, combative, opinionated. She wasn't feminine or frivolous or helpless and didn't need him for anything. It seemed clear to Alistair that they could never have a future together, even if Morgan were prepared to consider it. Their lives were just too different.

Shelley had seen that. Her admiration for Morgan had reminded him of all the things he had let himself forget. When he was thinking about the way that nightdress had skimmed over her body, when he was noticing the curve of her mouth and the pure line of her throat, he should have been remembering that she was a phenomenally successful businesswoman. She was attractive and assured. She was clever and capable and *rich*.

She wasn't for him.

Their lives might have touched briefly, but now Shelley had gone they would continue inexorably on their separate trajectories.

Alistair told himself that would be for the best. Life would be much easier if Morgan wasn't there, making his senses reel, challenging him and confusing him and turning his steady, comfortable world upside down. He had been perfectly happy without her. Alistair wanted things to go back to the way they had been before Morgan had kissed him and changed everything.

'I'll tell anyone who asks that you're out of my league,' he told her. 'That's true, anyway. No one will have any difficulty believing that I'm not good enough for you.'

Morgan winced. That was what Paul had said too. *I'm not good enough for you. You deserve someone better.*

'Why don't we just say that we made a mutual decision that it wasn't going to work out?' she suggested in a colourless voice.

'We can do that if you like,' said Alistair. 'It's got the advantage of being true in a way too, hasn't it?'

'Yes,' Morgan agreed dully, because what else could she say? 'It's true.'

Saying goodbye was terrible. Alistair was grim, Polly and Phoebe tearful and the dogs confused.

'What happened?' Phoebe asked in a watery voice. 'We thought you and Dad were happy together.'

'Have you had an argument?' Polly was as wobbly and confused as her twin. 'Won't he say he's sorry? We could make him!'

Morgan swallowed. She couldn't hurt the girls now by telling them that it had all been a lie. That would make this even worse for them. 'It's nothing like that,' she said. 'It's something your Dad and I have decided together.'

'But *why*?' Phoebe wailed. 'Don't you love Dad any more?'

'It's…complicated,' said Morgan with difficulty. 'Sometimes things just don't work out the
way you hope they will. Your Dad did tell you
that you would only be here for a while, until we
decided whether we wanted to make it permanent or not,' she reminded them, throat aching
with the effort of not crying too. 'Don't be sad.
We'll still be friends.'

'But we'll miss you.' Both girls clung to her
waist. 'Can we still come and see you?'

'Of course you can.' Morgan hugged them
tightly to her. 'Come any time.'

Letting them go was one of the hardest things
she had ever done. Morgan stood on the steps,
clutching her arms together, and watched Alistair
load up the car with reluctant children and
animals. She had used to think that a broken
heart was just a metaphor, but right then hers felt
as if someone had taken it in a cruel grip and
twisted and torn it apart, leaving a gaping,
bloody wound that was so painful she could
hardly breathe.

Tallulah was at her feet, puzzled by the change
in routine, and Morgan bent to pick her up,
hugging her close for the illusion of comfort as
Alistair reversed back past her Porsche, lifted a

hand in farewell, and drove off down the long drive back to his life in Ingleton where there was no place for her and where she didn't belong.

The twins came back as promised two days later. 'We wanted to come yesterday but Dad says we can't come every day,' they complained to Morgan.

'He's really, really grumpy at the moment,' Polly confided.

'We miss you,' Phoebe added. 'And Bert and Tip miss Tallulah. We asked if we could come back and live with you, and he *shouted* at us.' Her small face blackened with remembered outrage. 'He told us there was no question of it and we weren't to mention it again, but I don't see why. It's not fair. We were happy here with you, and you were happy too, weren't you?'

Morgan's heart twisted. 'Yes,' she said. 'I was.'

But, as the days passed, it grew harder and harder to remember what happiness was. Morgan knew what she had to do. How many times in the past had she squared her shoulders, pushed her disappointment to the back of her mind and thrown herself into a new project to distract herself from thinking too much about the ache in her heart? She had done it before; she could do it again.

Hadn't she always been famous for her strength? For her pride? For her gritty determination and her ability to pick herself up, dust herself down and start all over again? Not this time. Morgan felt as if a great boot of misery had been planted on her back, pinning her to the ground and pressing her face into the dirt, and she couldn't have shaken it off and heaved herself to her feet if she had tried.

It wasn't even as if she had been rejected after a passionate affair, she tried to reason with herself. You couldn't call two kisses—neither of them real—a relationship. Alistair had promised nothing beyond the deal they had made. He had given her no reason to think that they might have a future together.

Minty worried about her. With a twin's intuition, she had rung the night Alistair left and she had known the truth the moment she heard Morgan's voice. Now she called to check up on Morgan every day.

'Why don't you just *talk* to Alistair?' she asked in exasperation. 'Tell him how you feel.'

'I can't,' said Morgan flatly. 'I told you what he said to the girls. There's no question of them coming back.'

'Maybe you could go to them?' suggested Minty, but Morgan wouldn't hear of it.

'No, I'm giving up on relationships,' she told her sister one day. She had decided in the night that it was time to get off the ground, and if she hadn't quite made it to her feet, at least she was on her knees. 'I'm sick of feeling miserable. I'm going back to work.'

Minty didn't think much of that idea. 'It's not your company any more,' she pointed out.

'I'm going to start a consultancy,' said Morgan. 'I thought I could help people set up local businesses. I could offer financial and practical advice about starting a company. I might even invest if I think there's real potential there.'

'As long as you don't get obsessed with work again,' said Minty dubiously. 'You know what you're like.'

'And I'm going to sell Ingleton Hall.'

Minty was horrified. 'Morgan, you can't! You love that house.'

'It's got too many memories now, Minty. I can't bear it any more. I'll move to York or Harrogate…anywhere I don't spend my time being terrified that I might bump into Alistair without being prepared and then feeling bitterly disappointed because I never do. Anyway, I've made up my mind,' said Morgan before her sister could come up with any more objections. 'The valuers are coming tomorrow.'

At last she was on the road to recovery, Morgan congratulated herself as she switched off the phone. She had a plan—two plans, in fact—so she had no excuse now not to move on, put Alistair and her brief experience of being part of a family behind her, and get used to being on her own again.

If only it were that easy. Morgan put Ingleton Hall on the market and drew up some initial plans for her new consultancy, but her life was still bleak and desolate, her heart still raw with longing and regret for the happiness she had so nearly found.

She struggled from one day to the next, each spent marking time until she could fall into bed and the oblivion of sleep. In an attempt to physically exhaust herself, Morgan took to taking Tallulah for long walks. The little dog was getting positively trim, but even that silver lining brought bittersweet memories of the first time she had met Alistair. Everything reminded her of him.

Shoulders hunched, head bent against the drizzle, Morgan trudged up the drive one damp, dreary July day. The weather matched her spirits, but Tallulah, who had always hated the rain, was trailing sulkily behind. Almost at the house, Morgan stopped and waited for her to catch up and, as she turned back, she lifted her head and saw the car parked beside hers for the first time, its battered and mud-splashed appearance throwing the pristine, gleaming lines of the Porsche into sharp relief.

It was Alistair's.

Her heart gave a great lurch and started battering painfully against her ribs and she had to draw a long, shaky breath before she could trust herself to walk on. The back doors had flown open and Polly and Phoebe were hurtling down the drive towards her, followed by the dogs, who were barking excitably.

Polly reached Morgan first and made her stagger as she threw herself into Morgan's arms. 'Morgan, don't go! You can't go!'

'Yes, please don't go.' Phoebe clutched at Morgan's waist, her small face puckered with the effort of not crying.

'Get back in the car, girls.' Alistair's voice sliced through the sound of Polly and Phoebe's tearful demands and of the over-excited dogs.

Morgan looked over the twins' heads to see him striding down the drive after his family. He looked very angry. There was a rigid set to his shoulders and his mouth was compressed in a straight line, his grey eyes stony.

'We wanted to see Morgan,' Phoebe began, but he cut her off.

'Do as I say,' he said curtly. 'Go on, both of you. This is between Morgan and me.'

When their father spoke like that, the girls obeyed. Reluctantly relinquishing their hold on Morgan, they trailed back to the car. 'Be nice to her,' Polly shouted tearfully over her shoulder. 'You're *horrid* at the moment!'

Alistair ignored his daughters. Taking Morgan by the arm, he steered her not very gently out of earshot. 'What's going on?' he demanded.

'I think that's *my* question!' Morgan finally succeeded in shaking her arm free.

That first instinctive leap of joy she had felt at the sight of him was being rapidly consumed by a flickering flame of anger. It was weeks since they had last spoken and he couldn't even manage a hello!

This wasn't how she had imagined meeting Alistair again. In her fantasies, his face had lit at the sight of her. He had swept her into his arms and told her how much he had missed her. He certainly hadn't barked orders at his children, grabbed her arm and frogmarched her under the shelter of a tree. He hadn't glared at her as if he hated her.

So much for fantasies.

'Is it true that you're selling Ingleton Hall?'

'How did you hear that?'

'I went home this afternoon to find Polly and Phoebe in tears. I don't know who told them, and it doesn't matter. I just want to know if it's true or not.'

Morgan rubbed her arm where he had gripped her. 'Yes, it's true.'

'And you never thought to tell me?' Alistair was very white about the mouth.

'To be honest, Alistair, I'd no reason to believe that you were remotely interested in what I was doing,' said Morgan coldly, although inside she was trembling violently. 'I haven't seen you or heard from you in six weeks.'

'You've seen the girls,' he countered. 'How did you think they would feel when they heard you were planning to up and off without a word to them?'

'I was going to say goodbye,' she protested.

'Oh, and that would make it OK, would it?' said Alistair furiously. 'You think you can just say "bye" and abandon us all?'

Morgan flinched at the very word. 'I would never abandon anyone,' she said in a low, shaking voice. 'You know that.'

'Well, that's how it feels!' he told her flatly. 'Do you have any idea how much the girls are going to miss you?'

'They might miss my pool,' said Morgan with a touch of bitterness. 'Not me.'

'Yes, *you*,' Alistair insisted. 'Of course they'll miss you.'

Involuntarily, Morgan glanced towards the car, where two anxious little faces were pressed against the window, watching them. There was an iron hand gripping her throat and she couldn't bear to look back at them.

'I'll miss them, too,' she muttered.

In the background Bert and Tip were attempting to frolic with Tallulah, who was in no mood for a joyful reunion. The drizzle had eased off by then, but she was still cross and barked irritably as they bounced around her.

Alistair, apparently in no better temper,

shouted across at the dogs to be quiet, then turned back to Morgan, who was standing watching him with great wary dark eyes, and all at once the anger that had consumed him since he'd first heard that she was leaving without letting him know evaporated without warning.

'You know, Tip and Bert will miss you as well,' he said softly.

Something had changed in his voice. Morgan didn't know what it was, but it gave her the courage to look directly back at him. 'And you?' she asked, lifting her chin in a gesture so familiar that Alistair felt his heart contract.

'I'll miss you most of all,' he said.

All the breath leaked out of Morgan's lungs. 'You will?'

'Of course I will!' There was an edge of exasperation in his voice now. 'Morgan, do you have *any* idea what you've done to me?' he asked her. 'You've turned my world upside down!'

'I haven't done anything!'

'Oh, yes, you have,' he corrected her. 'You've been yourself. You've been prickly and funny and warm and beautiful and argumentative, and I've been through hell just trying to keep my hands off you!'

Astounded, Morgan opened her mouth, failed to think of anything to say, and shut it again.

'You got under my skin,' Alistair told her. 'The last thing I wanted was to fall in love with you. It was the last thing I expected, too, and for a long time I told myself that I didn't really love you at all. How could I love you? You were totally unlike anyone I could ever imagine loving. I told myself that we were too different, that it could never work even if you were interested, that you could never love me…'

He lifted his shoulders in a helpless gesture, wondering if he could possibly make Morgan understand. 'So I took the girls and went home and tried to forget you, but I couldn't do it. We were all so miserable without you. The girls were moping, the dogs pining, and I couldn't settle to anything. It wasn't home any more because you weren't there,' he said.

'I've been in a foul temper,' he admitted. 'Polly was right, I *have* been horrid! But the more I missed you, the more angry I got that I couldn't accept the inevitable—that you would never be interested in someone like me—and forget about the few weeks we'd spent together. I wanted to forget that I knew what it was like to kiss you. I wanted to forget all about you and find someone more suitable. I wanted to move on.'

Alistair paused, his mouth twisting in an ironic smile. 'And then when I heard today that you were doing just that, when I hadn't been able to, I was so furious that I didn't think at all. Bodil's gone back to Sweden, so I just put the girls in the car and came up here to see you.

'And now I'm here,' he said, his voice deepening, 'and you're standing right in front of me, and suddenly I don't know why I was so angry. I can't remember what I wanted to say to you,' he went on. 'I just know that I'm so pleased just to see you again, I don't know what to do with myself!'

Morgan stared at him, hardly daring to believe what he was saying. 'I don't understand,' she said slowly. 'Why did you go if you felt like that?'

'I assumed that was what you wanted,' said Alistair. 'You'd never indicated that you wanted anything more, and I wasn't surprised. You've got so much, Morgan. I don't mean money,' he said as she made an impatient gesture. 'I mean talent and drive and intelligence. You're an incredible person. You deserve so much better.'

'Better than what?' asked Morgan.

'Better than anything I could ever offer you,' he said. 'All I've got to offer you is a family.'

'Maybe a family is what I want,' she said softly.

'Is it?' Hope dawning in his heart, Alistair reached out and took her hands in his. 'You might find another family, Morgan. You might even find one that deserves you more, but you won't find one that needs you more, or loves you more, than we do. Because it's not just me that loves you. My daughters do and my dogs do, too.' His grasp was warm and secure and incredibly reassuring. 'Is there any chance at all that you would think about hiring us again as a family?'

'You mean on a temporary basis again?'

'Well, no,' said Alistair, his grip tightening in response to the smile he could see trembling on Morgan's lips. 'We're looking for a permanent position this time.'

'And what exactly are you offering?'

'Polly and Phoebe would make sure your pool was adequately used,' he pointed out, an answering smile dawning in his grey eyes. 'And they'd keep you busy elsewhere, too. We wouldn't want you getting bored, after all. You'd have to take the dogs out, too, because they like walking with you, and that would keep you fit.'

Morgan pretended to consider as her fingers curled around his. 'Hmm...that does sound like a tempting offer,' she said.

'Then there's me,' said Alistair. 'I'd run you a bath when you're tired, and rub your back when you're stiff. I'd make you laugh when you're down and I'd argue with you when you're up, and I'd be so proud of you always because of who you are and what you've achieved.'

'Is that it?' Morgan asked, primming her mouth and trying to look unconvinced, which was hard when her heart was singing and happiness was fizzing along her veins like champagne.

'No, that's just the start,' he said. 'I'd love you for ever and want you for ever and make love to you for ever.'

'Ah,' sighed Morgan, deeply pleased. 'That's more like it!' She couldn't hold back the smile any longer. 'Well, it all sounds very interesting but, as you know, I'm a hard-headed business-woman. I'd need to know how you would expect to be paid for all this,' she said, and Alistair grinned as he drew her closer.

'In kind,' he promised, and then he could kiss

her at last, a long, long hungry kiss to make up
for the all the times they had never been able to
kiss like this before.

Morgan melted into him and kissed him back,
feeling the last of the black misery trickle away,
vanquished in a great rolling wash of relief and
joy and giddy exhilaration.

'I love you,' she said raggedly when they eventually broke for breath. Pulling away slightly so
that she could look into his face, she smiled up
at him. 'I love you,' she said again, because it
was so wonderful just to be able to say it, to be
able to touch him and hold him close and know
that this time it was for real and that she never
had to let him go.

'I love you, too,' said Alistair, needing her back
in his arms, wanting to kiss her again and again.

The dogs were barking, thoroughly over-
excited, and the next moment the car doors banged
and, unable to contain themselves any longer,
Phoebe and Polly came running across the gravel.

'Dad, Dad, is everything OK now?'

Alistair smiled as he lifted his head, but he
didn't let Morgan go. 'Yes,' he said. 'Everything's perfect.'

'Does that mean we can come home?'

Morgan nodded, her eyes shimmering with tears of joy. 'You are home,' she said.

The girls whooped and threw themselves at their father and Morgan, sending the dogs into even more of a frenzy with their shrieks of happiness. Even Tallulah allowed herself to be caught up in the excitement and ran around in hysterical circles with Bert.

'We *knew* you were perfect for each other!' said Phoebe exultantly.

Polly nodded vigorous agreement as she hugged Morgan. 'You see, we were right all along,' she pointed out. 'Dad told us not to matchmake, but if we hadn't invited you to tea, you would never have met, would you?'

'That's true,' said Morgan, tactfully not pointing out that she and Alistair had already met before the invitation to tea. Let them have their moment of glory, though. 'We'd have been in a right old muddle without you two.'

'And we *told* Dad he should have come and talked to you ages ago,' Phoebe added. 'Didn't we, Dad?'

'You did,' he agreed. 'At length!'

'You should have listened to us,' they said triumphantly.

'Girls,' Morgan interjected. 'How would you like a swim?'

She thought it might be too obvious a distraction, but their faces lit up. 'Can we?'

Alistair laughed ruefully as they raced off. 'They're going to be unbearable,' he said, resigned, and drew Morgan back into his arms. 'The worst thing is, they *were* right. They knew just what I needed and that you were the perfect woman for me long before I did.'

'Alistair?' Morgan put her palms on his chest and held him away a little. There was just one thing that she wanted to be sure about. 'Are you sure you don't want me just because it makes Phoebe and Polly so happy?'

He looked down into her face and wondered anew that someone like Morgan could have so little confidence in herself. She had no idea how beautiful she was, how much he wanted her. Well, that was OK, Alistair told himself. He had a lifetime to convince her.

'Are *you* sure you're not taking me back just because you miss the girls?' he countered.

'Of course not,' said Morgan indignantly. 'I really miss the dogs, too.'

For a split second Alistair wondered if she was

serious, then he saw the gleam of mischief in her dark eyes and he laughed. 'I guess I deserved that!' he said. 'And there was me hoping that it was me that you missed.'

'I did.' Morgan's smile faded. 'I missed you more than you'll ever know. It's you that I want, Alistair, but I know that you don't come on your own. The girls and the dogs are part of the package. I can't have you without your family, and I wouldn't want that anyway. All I want is to be part of that family, too.'

Alistair took her face very tenderly between his hands and looked deep into her brown eyes. 'You are part of it,' he said, kissing her softly. 'We're not a proper family without you. Will you marry me, Morgan, and make it official? I'm afraid nothing less than a wedding will do for the twins!'

'Oh, well, if it's what Polly and Phoebe want …
then yes,' said Morgan, smiling as she relaxed blissfully into a long, sweet kiss, 'I will!'

It was some time later before they made their way into the house to find the twins. 'We'll tell them that we're getting married soon,' said Alistair, his arm around Morgan. 'Maybe that'll keep them quiet.'

'I suppose this means I don't have to hire a

family anymore,' said Morgan happily, and Alistair stopped to kiss her again.

'No,' he said. 'We're not a family for hire now. We're a family for ever.'

MILLS & BOON® PUBLISH EIGHT LARGE PRINT TITLES A MONTH. THESE ARE THE EIGHT TITLES FOR OCTOBER 2006

PRINCE OF THE DESERT
Penny Jordan

FOR PLEASURE...OR MARRIAGE?
Julia James

THE ITALIAN'S PRICE
Diana Hamilton

THE JET-SET SEDUCTION
Sandra Field

HER OUTBACK PROTECTOR
Margaret Way

THE SHEIKH'S SECRET
Barbara McMahon

A WOMAN WORTH LOVING
Jackie Braun

HER READY-MADE FAMILY
Jessica Hart

0906 R€

MILLS & BOON® PUBLISH EIGHT LARGE PRINT TITLES A MONTH. THESE ARE THE EIGHT TITLES FOR NOVEMBER 2006

———— ❧ ————

THE SECRET BABY REVENGE
Emma Darcy

THE PRINCE'S VIRGIN WIFE
Lucy Monroe

TAKEN FOR HIS PLEASURE
Carol Marinelli

AT THE GREEK TYCOON'S BIDDING
Cathy Williams

THE HEIR'S CHOSEN BRIDE
Marion Lennox

THE MILLIONAIRE'S CINDERELLA WIFE
Lilian Darcy

THEIR UNFINISHED BUSINESS
Jackie Braun

THE TYCOON'S PROPOSAL
Leigh Michaels

MILLS & BOON®

Live the emotion

1006 Rom LP